IN THE BELFRY.

Otto

Of the Silver Hand

Otto

Of the Silver Hand

Written and Illustrated by
HOWARD PYLE

ISBN: 978-93-5128-535-9

First Published in 1914
Indian Reprint in 2017

Published by

Kalpaz Publications
C-30, Satyawati Nagar,
Delhi – 110052
E-mail: kalpaz@hotmail.com
Website: kalpazpublications.com
Ph.: +91-9212142040

Cataloging in Publication Data—DK
Courtesy: D.K. Agencies (P) Ltd. <docinfo@dkagencies.com>

Pyle, Howard, 1853-1911, author.
Otto of the silver hand / written and illustrated by Howard Pyle.
pages cm
Children's stories.
"First published in 1914"—Title page verso.
ISBN 9789351285359

1. Children—Conduct of life—Juvenile fiction. 2. Fathers and sons—Juvenile fiction. 3. Middle ages—Juvenile fiction. 4. Children's stories, American. I. Title.

PZ7.P993Ot 2017 DDC 813.4 23

CONTENTS

Foreword

Between the far away past history of the world, and that which lies near to us; in the time when the wisdom of the ancient times was dead and had passed away, and our own days of light had not yet come, there lay a great black gulf in human history, a gulf of ignorance, of superstition, of cruelty, and of wickedness.

That time we call the dark or middle ages.

Few records remain to us of that dreadful period in our world's history, and we only know of it through broken and disjointed fragments that have been handed down to us through the generations.

Yet, though the world's life then was so wicked and black, there yet remained a few good men and women here and there (mostly in peaceful and quiet monasteries, far from the thunder and the glare of the worlds bloody battle), who knew the right and the truth and lived according to what they knew; who preserved and tenderly cared for the truths that the dear Christ taught, and lived and died for in Palestine so long ago.

This tale that I am about to tell is of a little boy who lived and suffered in those dark middle ages; of how he saw both the good and the bad of men, and of how, by gentleness and love and not by strife and hatred, he came at last to stand above other men and to be looked up to by all. And should you follow the story to the end, I hope you may find it a pleasure, as I have done, to ramble through those dark ancient castles, to lie with little Otto and Brother John in the high belfry-tower, or to sit with them in the peaceful quiet of the sunny old monastery garden, for, of all the story, I love best those early peaceful years that little Otto spent in the dear old White Cross on the Hill.

Poor little Otto's life was a stony and a thorny pathway, and it is well for all of us nowadays that we walk it in fancy and not in truth.

Chapter - I

The Dragon's House

Up from the gray rocks, rising sheer and bold and bare, stood the walls and towers of Castle Drachenhausen. A great gate-way, with a heavy iron-pointed portcullis hanging suspended in the dim arch above, yawned blackly upon the bascule or falling drawbridge that spanned a chasm between the blank stone walls and the roadway that winding down the steep rocky slope to the little valley just beneath. There in the lap of the hills around stood the wretched straw-thatched huts of the peasants belonging to the castle - miserable serfs who, half timid, half fierce, tilled their poor patches of ground, wrenching from the hard soil barely enough to keep body and soul together. Among those vile hovels played the little children like foxes about their dens, their wild, fierce eyes peering out from under a mat of tangled yellow hair.

Beyond these squalid huts lay the rushing, foaming river, spanned by a high, rude, stone bridge where the road from the castle crossed it, and beyond the river stretched the great, black forest, within whose gloomy depths the savage wild beasts made their lair, and where in winter time the howling wolves coursed their flying prey across the moonlit snow and under the net-work of the black shadows from the naked boughs above.

The watchman in the cold, windy bartizan or watch-tower that clung to the gray walls above the castle gateway, looked from his narrow window, where the wind piped and hummed, across the tree-tops that rolled in endless billows of green, over hill and over valley to the blue and distant slope of the Keiserberg, where, on the mountain side, glimmered far away the walls of Castle Trutz-Drachen.

THERE THEY SAT, JUST AS LITTLE CHILDREN IN THE TOWN MIGHT SIT UPON THEIR FATHER'S DOOR-STEP.

Within the massive stone walls through which the gaping gateway led, three great cheerless brick buildings, so forbidding that even the yellow sunlight could not light them into brightness, looked down, with row upon row of windows, upon three sides of the bleak, stone courtyard. Back of and above them clustered a jumble of other buildings, tower and turret, one high-peaked roof overtopping another.

The great house in the centre was the Baron's Hall, the part to the left was called the Roderhausen; between the two stood a huge square pile, rising dizzily up into the clear air high above the rest - the great Melchior Tower.

At the top clustered a jumble of buildings hanging high aloft in the windy space a crooked wooden belfry, a tall, narrow watch- tower, and a rude wooden house that clung partly to the roof of the great tower and partly to the walls.

From the chimney of this crazy hut a thin thread of smoke would now and then rise into the air, for there were folk living far up in that empty, airy desert, and oftentimes wild, uncouth little children were seen playing on the edge of the dizzy height, or sitting with their bare legs hanging down over the sheer depths, as they gazed below at what was going on in the court-yard. There they sat, just as little children in the town might sit upon their father's door-step; and as the sparrows might fly around the feet of the little town children, so the circling flocks of rooks and daws flew around the feet of these air-born creatures.

It was Schwartz Carl and his wife and little ones who lived far up there in the Melchior Tower, for it overlooked the top of the hill behind the castle and so down into the valley upon the further side. There, day after day, Schwartz Carl kept watch upon the gray road that ran like a ribbon through the valley, from the rich town of Gruenstaldt to the rich town of Staffenburgen, where passed merchant caravans from the one to the other - for the lord of Drachenhausen was a robber baron.

Dong! Dong! The great alarm bell would suddenly ring out from the belfry high up upon the Melchior Tower. Dong! Dong! Till the rooks and daws whirled clamoring and screaming. Dong! Dong! Till the fierce wolf-hounds in the rocky kennels behind the castle stables howled dismally in answer. Dong! Dong! - Dong! Dong!

Then would follow a great noise and uproar and hurry in the castle court-yard below; men shouting and calling to one another, the ringing of armor, and the clatter of horses' hoofs upon the hard stone. With the creaking and groaning of the windlass the iron-pointed portcullis would be slowly raised, and with a clank and rattle and clash of iron chains the drawbridge would fall crashing. Then over it would thunder horse and man, clattering away down the winding, stony pathway, until the great forest would swallow them, and they would be gone.

Then for a while peace would fall upon the castle courtyard, the cock would crow, the cook would scold a lazy maid, and Gretchen, leaning out of a window, would sing a snatch of a song, just as though it were a peaceful farm-house, instead of a den of robbers.

Maybe it would be evening before the men would return once more. Perhaps one would have a bloody cloth bound about his head, perhaps one would carry his arm in a sling; perhaps one - maybe more than one - would be left behind, never to return again, and soon forgotten by all excepting some poor woman who would weep silently in the loneliness of her daily work.

Nearly always the adventurers would bring back with them pack- horses laden with bales of goods. Sometimes, besides these, they would return with a poor soul, his hands tied behind his back and his feet beneath the horse's body, his fur cloak and his flat cap wofully awry. A while he would disappear in some gloomy cell of the dungeon-keep, until an envoy would come from the town with a fat purse, when his ransom would be paid, the dungeon would disgorge him, and he would be allowed to go upon his way again.

One man always rode beside Baron Conrad in his expeditions and adventures a short, deep-chested, broad-shouldered man, with sinewy arms so long that when he stood his hands hung nearly to his knees.

His coarse, close-clipped hair came so low upon his brow that only a strip of forehead showed between it and his bushy, black eyebrows. One eye was blind; the other twinkled and gleamed like a spark under the penthouse of his brows. Many folk said that the one-eyed Hans had drunk beer with the Hill-man, who had given him the strength of ten, for he could bend an iron spit like a hazel twig, and could lift a barrel of wine from the floor to his head as easily as though it were a basket of eggs.

As for the one-eyed Hans he never said that he had not drunk beer with the Hill-man, for he liked the credit that such reports gave him with the other folk. And so, like a half savage mastiff, faithful to death to his master, but to him alone, he went his sullen way and lived his sullen life within the castle walls, half respected, half feared by the other inmates, for it was dangerous trifling with the one-eyed Hans.

Chapter - II

How the Baron went Forth to Shear

Baron Conrad and Baroness Matilda sat together at their morning meal below their raised seats stretched the long, heavy wooden table, loaded with coarse food - black bread, boiled cabbage, bacon, eggs, a great chine from a wild boar, sausages, such as we eat nowadays, and flagons and jars of beer and wine, Along the board sat ranged in the order of the household the followers and retainers. Four or five slatternly women and girls served the others as they fed noisily at the table, moving here and there behind the men with wooden or pewter dishes of food, now and then laughing at the jests that passed or joining in the talk. A huge fire blazed and crackled and roared in the great open fireplace, before which were stretched two fierce, shaggy, wolfish-looking hounds. Outside, the rain beat upon the roof or ran trickling from the eaves, and every now and then a chill draught of wind would breathe through the open windows of the great black dining-hall and set the fire roaring.

Along the dull-gray wall of stone hung pieces of armor, and swords and lances, and great branching antlers of the stag. Overhead arched the rude, heavy, oaken beams, blackened with age and smoke, and underfoot was a chill pavement of stone.

Upon Baron Conrad's shoulder leaned the pale, slender, yellow- haired Baroness, the only one in all the world with whom the fierce lord of Drachenhausen softened to gentleness, the only one upon whom his savage brows looked kindly, and to whom his harsh voice softened with love.

The Baroness was talking to her husband in a low voice, as he looked down into her pale face, with its gentle blue eyes.

"And wilt thou not, then," said she, "do that one thing for me?"

"Nay," he growled, in his deep voice, "I cannot promise thee never more to attack the towns-people in the valley over yonder. How else could I live an' I did not take from the fat town hogs to fill our own larder?"

"Nay," said the Baroness, "thou couldst live as some others do, for all do not rob the burgher folk as thou dost. Alas! mishap will come upon thee some day, and if thou shouldst be slain, what then would come of me?"

"Prut," said the Baron, "thy foolish fears" But he laid his rough, hairy hand softly upon the Baroness' head and stroked her yellow hair.

"For my sake, Conrad," whispered the Baroness.

A pause followed. The Baron sat looking thoughtfully down into the Baroness' face. A moment more, and he might have promised what she besought; a moment more, and he might have been saved all the bitter trouble that was to follow. But it was not to be.

Suddenly a harsh sound broke the quietness of all into a confusion of noises. Dong! Dong! - it was the great alarm-bell from Melchior's Tower.

The Baron started at the sound. He sat for a moment or two with his hand clinched upon the arm of his seat as though about to rise, then he sunk back into his chair again.

All the others had risen tumultuously from the table, and now stood looking at him, awaiting his orders.

"For my sake, Conrad," said the Baroness again.

Dong! Dong! rang the alarm-bell. The Baron sat with his eyes bent upon the floor, scowling blackly.

The Baroness took his hand in both of hers. "For my sake," she pleaded, and the tears filled her blue eyes as she looked up at him, "do not go this time."

From the courtyard without came the sound of horses' hoofs clashing against the stone pavement, and those in the hall stood watching and wondering at this strange delay of the Lord Baron. Just then the door opened and one came pushing past the rest; it was the one-eyed Hans. He came straight to where the Baron sat, and, leaning over, whispered something into his master's ear.

"For my sake," implored the Baroness again; but the scale was turned. The Baron pushed back his chair heavily and rose to his feet. "Forward!" he roared, in a voice of thunder, and a great shout went up in answer as he strode clanking down the hall and out of the open door.

The Baroness covered her face with her hands and wept.

"Never mind, little bird," said old Ursela, the nurse, soothingly; "he will come back to thee again as he has come back to thee before."

But the poor young Baroness continued weeping with her face buried in her hands, because he had not done that thing she had asked.

AWAY THEY RODE WITH CLASHING HOOFS AND RINGING ARMOR.

A white young face framed in yellow hair looked out into the courtyard from a window above; but if Baron Conrad of Drachenhausen saw it from beneath the bars of his shining helmet, he made no sign.

"Forward" he cried again.

Down thundered the drawbridge, and away they rode with clashing hoofs and ringing armor through the gray shroud of drilling rain.

The day had passed and the evening had come, and the Baroness and her women sat beside a roaring fire. All were chattering and talking and laughing but two - the fair young Baroness and old Ursela; the one sat listening, listening, listening, the other sat with her chin resting in the palm of her hand, silently watching her young mistress. The night was falling gray and chill, when suddenly the clear notes of a bugle rang from without the castle walls. The young Baroness started, and the rosy light flashed up into her pale cheeks.

"Yes, good," said old Ursela; "the red fox has come back to his den again, and I warrant he brings a fat town goose in his mouth; now we'll have fine clothes to wear, and thou another gold chain to hang about thy pretty neck."

The young Baroness laughed merrily at the old woman's speech. "This time," said she, "I will choose a string of pearls like that one my aunt used to wear, and which I had about my neck when Conrad first saw me."

Minute after minute passed; the Baroness sat nervously playing with a bracelet of golden beads about her wrist. "How long he stays," said she.

"Yes," said Ursela; "but it is not cousin wish that holds him by the coat."

As she spoke, a door banged in the passageway without, and the ring of iron footsteps sounded upon the stone floor. Clank! Clank! Clank!

The Baroness rose to her feet, her face all alight. The door opened; then the flush of joy faded away and the face grew white, white, white. One hand clutched the back of the bench whereon she had been sitting, the other hand pressed tightly against her side.

It was Hans the one-eyed who stood in the doorway, and black trouble sat on his brow; all were looking at him waiting.

"Conrad," whispered the Baroness, at last. "Where is Conrad? Where is your master?" and even her lips were white as she spoke.

The one-eyed Hans said nothing.

Just then came the noise of men s voices in the corridor and the shuffle and scuffle of feet carrying a heavy load. Nearer and nearer they came, and one-eyed Hans stood aside. Six men came struggling through the doorway, carrying a litter, and on the litter lay the great Baron Conrad. The flaming torch thrust into the iron bracket against the wall flashed up with the draught of air from the open door, and the light fell upon the white face and the closed eyes, and showed upon his body armor a great red stain that was not the stain of rust.

Otto

Of the Silver Hand

Otto

Of the Silver Hand

Written and Illustrated by

HOWARD PYLE

ISBN: 978-93-5128-535-9

First Published in 1914
Indian Reprint in 2017

Published by

Kalpaz Publications
C-30, Satyawati Nagar,
Delhi – 110052
E-mail: kalpaz@hotmail.com
Website: kalpazpublications.com
Ph.: +91-9212142040

Cataloging in Publication Data—DK
Courtesy: D.K. Agencies (P) Ltd. <docinfo@dkagencies.com>

Pyle, Howard, 1853-1911, author.
Otto of the silver hand / written and illustrated by Howard Pyle.
pages cm
Children's stories.
"First published in 1914"—Title page verso.
ISBN 9789351285359

1. Children—Conduct of life—Juvenile fiction. 2. Fathers and sons—Juvenile fiction. 3. Middle ages—Juvenile fiction. 4. Children's stories, American. I. Title.

PZ7.P993Ot 2017 DDC 813.4 23

"Where is your lady?" said the Baron again, in the same hoarse voice; and then, not waiting for an answer, "Is she dead?"

The old woman looked at him for a minute blinking her watery eyes, and then suddenly broke into a shrill, long-drawn wail. The Baron needed to hear no more.

As though in answer to the old woman's cry, a thin piping complaint came from the bundle in her lap.

At the sound the red blood flashed up into the Baron's face. "What is that you have there?" said he, pointing to the bundle upon the old woman's knees.

She drew back the coverings and there lay a poor, weak, little baby, that once again raised its faint reedy pipe.

"It is your son," said Ursela, "that the dear Baroness left behind her when the holy angels took her to Paradise. She blessed him and called him Otto before she left us."

Chapter - IV

The White Cross on the Hill

Here the glassy waters of the River Rhine, holding upon its bosom a mimic picture of the blue sky and white clouds floating above, runs smoothly around a jutting point of land, St. Michaelsburg, rising from the reedy banks of the stream, sweeps up with a smooth swell until it cuts sharp and clear against the sky. Stubby vineyards covered its earthy breast, and field and garden and orchard crowned its brow, where lay the Monastery of St. Michaelsburg - "The White Cross on the Hill." There within the white walls, where the warm yellow sunlight slept, all was peaceful quietness, broken only now and then by the crowing of the cock or the clamorous cackle of a hen, the lowing of kine or the bleating of goats, a solitary voice in prayer, the faint accord of distant singing, or the resonant toll of the monastery bell from the high-peaked belfry that overlooked the hill and valley and the smooth, far-winding stream. No other sounds broke the stillness, for in this peaceful haven was never heard the clash of armor, the ring of iron-shod hoofs, or the hoarse call to arms.

All men were not wicked and cruel and fierce in that dark, far- away age; all were not robbers and terror-spreading tyrants, even in that time when men's hands were against their neighbors, and war and rapine dwelt in place of peace and justice.

Abbot Otto, of St. Michaelsburg, was a gentle, patient, pale. faced old man; his white hands were soft and smooth, and no one would have thought that they could have known the harsh touch of sword-hilt and lance. And yet, in the days of the Emperor Frederick - the grandson of the great Red-beard - no one stood higher in the prowess of arms than he. But all at once - for why,

ABBOT OTTO, OF ST. MICHAELSBURG, WAS A GENTLE, PATIENT, PALE-FACED OLD MAN.

no man could tell - a change came over him, and in the flower of his youth and fame and growing power he gave up everything in life and entered the quiet sanctuary of that white monastery on the hill-side, so far away from the tumult and the conflict of the world in which he had lived.

Some said that it was because the lady he had loved had loved his brother, and that when they were married Otto of Wolbergen had left the church with a broken heart.

But such stories are old songs that have been sung before.

Clatter! clatter! Jingle! jingle! It was a full-armed knight that came riding up the steep hill road that wound from left to right and right to left amid the vineyards on the slopes of St. Michaelsburg. Polished helm and corselet blazed in the noon sunlight, for no knight in those days dared to ride the roads except in full armor. In front of him the solitary knight carried a bundle wrapped in the folds of his coarse gray cloak.

It was a sorely sick man that rode up the heights of St. Michaelsburg. His head hung upon his breast through the faintness of weariness and pain; for it was the Baron Conrad.

He had left his bed of sickness that morning, had saddled his horse in the gray dawn with his own hands, and had ridden away into the misty twilight of the forest without the knowledge of anyone excepting the porter, who, winking and blinking in the bewilderment of his broken slumber, had opened the gates to the sick man, hardly knowing what he was doing, until he beheld his master far away, clattering down the steep bridle-path.

Eight leagues had he ridden that day with neither a stop nor a stay; but now at last the end of his journey had come, and he drew rein under the shade of the great wooden gateway of St. Michaelsburg.

He reached up to the knotted rope and gave it a pull, and from within sounded the answering ring of the porter's bell. By and by a little wicket opened in the great wooden portals, and the gentle, wrinkled face of old Brother Benedict, the porter, peeped out at the strange iron-clad visitor and the great black war-horse, streaked and wet with the sweat of the journey, flecked and dappled with flakes of foam. A few words passed between them, and then the little window was closed again; and within, the shuffling pat of the sandalled feet sounded fainter and fainter, as Brother Benedict bore the message from Baron Conrad to Abbot Otto, and the mail-clad figure was left alone, sitting there as silent as a statue.

By and by the footsteps sounded again; there came a noise of clattering chains and the rattle of the key in the lock, and the rasping of the bolts dragged back. Then the gate swung slowly open, and Baron Conrad rode into the shelter of the White Cross, and as the hoofs of his war-horse clashed upon the stones of the courtyard within, the wooden gate swung slowly to behind him.

Chapter - I

The Dragon's House

Up from the gray rocks, rising sheer and bold and bare, stood the walls and towers of Castle Drachenhausen. A great gate-way, with a heavy iron-pointed portcullis hanging suspended in the dim arch above, yawned blackly upon the bascule or falling drawbridge that spanned a chasm between the blank stone walls and the roadway that winding down the steep rocky slope to the little valley just beneath. There in the lap of the hills around stood the wretched straw-thatched huts of the peasants belonging to the castle - miserable serfs who, half timid, half fierce, tilled their poor patches of ground, wrenching from the hard soil barely enough to keep body and soul together. Among those vile hovels played the little children like foxes about their dens, their wild, fierce eyes peering out from under a mat of tangled yellow hair.

Beyond these squalid huts lay the rushing, foaming river, spanned by a high, rude, stone bridge where the road from the castle crossed it, and beyond the river stretched the great, black forest, within whose gloomy depths the savage wild beasts made their lair, and where in winter time the howling wolves coursed their flying prey across the moonlit snow and under the net-work of the black shadows from the naked boughs above.

The watchman in the cold, windy bartizan or watch-tower that clung to the gray walls above the castle gateway, looked from his narrow window, where the wind piped and hummed, across the tree-tops that rolled in endless billows of green, over hill and over valley to the blue and distant slope of the Keiserberg, where, on the mountain side, glimmered far away the walls of Castle Trutz-Drachen.

THERE THEY SAT, JUST AS LITTLE CHILDREN IN THE TOWN MIGHT SIT UPON THEIR FATHER'S DOOR-STEP.

Within the massive stone walls through which the gaping gateway led, three great cheerless brick buildings, so forbidding that even the yellow sunlight could not light them into brightness, looked down, with row upon row of windows, upon three sides of the bleak, stone courtyard. Back of and above them clustered a jumble of other buildings, tower and turret, one high-peaked roof overtopping another.

The great house in the centre was the Baron's Hall, the part to the left was called the Roderhausen; between the two stood a huge square pile, rising dizzily up into the clear air high above the rest - the great Melchior Tower.

At the top clustered a jumble of buildings hanging high aloft in the windy space a crooked wooden belfry, a tall, narrow watch- tower, and a rude wooden house that clung partly to the roof of the great tower and partly to the walls.

From the chimney of this crazy hut a thin thread of smoke would now and then rise into the air, for there were folk living far up in that empty, airy desert, and oftentimes wild, uncouth little children were seen playing on the edge of the dizzy height, or sitting with their bare legs hanging down over the sheer depths, as they gazed below at what was going on in the court-yard. There they sat, just as little children in the town might sit upon their father's door-step; and as the sparrows might fly around the feet of the little town children, so the circling flocks of rooks and daws flew around the feet of these air-born creatures.

It was Schwartz Carl and his wife and little ones who lived far up there in the Melchior Tower, for it overlooked the top of the hill behind the castle and so down into the valley upon the further side. There, day after day, Schwartz Carl kept watch upon the gray road that ran like a ribbon through the valley, from the rich town of Gruenstaldt to the rich town of Staffenburgen, where passed merchant caravans from the one to the other - for the lord of Drachenhausen was a robber baron.

Dong! Dong! The great alarm bell would suddenly ring out from the belfry high up upon the Melchior Tower. Dong! Dong! Till the rooks and daws whirled clamoring and screaming. Dong! Dong! Till the fierce wolf-hounds in the rocky kennels behind the castle stables howled dismally in answer. Dong! Dong! - Dong! Dong!

Then would follow a great noise and uproar and hurry in the castle court-yard below; men shouting and calling to one another, the ringing of armor, and the clatter of horses' hoofs upon the hard stone. With the creaking and groaning of the windlass the iron-pointed portcullis would be slowly raised, and with a clank and rattle and clash of iron chains the drawbridge would fall crashing. Then over it would thunder horse and man, clattering away down the winding, stony pathway, until the great forest would swallow them, and they would be gone.

Then for a while peace would fall upon the castle courtyard, the cock would crow, the cook would scold a lazy maid, and Gretchen, leaning out of a window, would sing a snatch of a song, just as though it were a peaceful farm-house, instead of a den of robbers.

Maybe it would be evening before the men would return once more. Perhaps one would have a bloody cloth bound about his head, perhaps one would carry his arm in a sling; perhaps one - maybe more than one - would be left behind, never to return again, and soon forgotten by all excepting some poor woman who would weep silently in the loneliness of her daily work.

Nearly always the adventurers would bring back with them pack- horses laden with bales of goods. Sometimes, besides these, they would return with a poor soul, his hands tied behind his back and his feet beneath the horse's body, his fur cloak and his flat cap wofully awry. A while he would disappear in some gloomy cell of the dungeon-keep, until an envoy would come from the town with a fat purse, when his ransom would be paid, the dungeon would disgorge him, and he would be allowed to go upon his way again.

One man always rode beside Baron Conrad in his expeditions and adventures a short, deep-chested, broad-shouldered man, with sinewy arms so long that when he stood his hands hung nearly to his knees.

His coarse, close-clipped hair came so low upon his brow that only a strip of forehead showed between it and his bushy, black eyebrows. One eye was blind; the other twinkled and gleamed like a spark under the penthouse of his brows. Many folk said that the one-eyed Hans had drunk beer with the Hill-man, who had given him the strength of ten, for he could bend an iron spit like a hazel twig, and could lift a barrel of wine from the floor to his head as easily as though it were a basket of eggs.

As for the one-eyed Hans he never said that he had not drunk beer with the Hill-man, for he liked the credit that such reports gave him with the other folk. And so, like a half savage mastiff, faithful to death to his master, but to him alone, he went his sullen way and lived his sullen life within the castle walls, half respected, half feared by the other inmates, for it was dangerous trifling with the one-eyed Hans.

Chapter - V

How Otto Dwelt at St. Michaelsburg

So the poor, little, motherless waif lived among the old monks at the White Cross on the hill, thriving and growing apace until he had reached eleven or twelve years of age; a slender, fair- haired little fellow, with a strange, quiet serious manner.

"Poor little child!" Old Brother Benedict would sometimes say to the others, "poor little child! The troubles in which he was born must have broken his wits like a glass cup. What think ye he said to me to-day? 'Dear Brother Benedict,' said he, 'dost thou shave the hair off of the top of thy head so that the dear God may see thy thoughts the better?' Think of that now!" and the good old man shook with silent laughter.

When such talk came to the good Father Abbot's ears, he smiled quietly to himself. "It may be," said he, "that the wisdom of little children flies higher than our heavy wits can follow."

At least Otto was not slow with his studies, and Brother Emmanuel, who taught him his lessons, said more than once that, if his wits were cracked in other ways, they were sound enough in Latin.

Otto, in a quaint, simple way which belonged to him, was gentle and obedient to all. But there was one among the Brethren of St. Michaelsburg whom he loved far above all the rest - Brother John, a poor half-witted fellow, of some twenty-five or thirty years of age. When a very little child, he had fallen from his nurse's arms and hurt his head, and as he grew up into boyhood, and showed that his wits had been addled by his fall, his family knew not what else to do with him, and so sent him off to the Monastery of St. Michaelsburg, where he lived his simple, witless life upon a sort of sufferance, as though he were a tame, harmless animal.

While Otto was still a little baby, he had been given into Brother John's care. Thereafter, and until Otto had grown old enough to care for himself, poor Brother John never left his little charge, night or day. Oftentimes the good Father Abbot, coming into the garden, where he loved to walk alone in his meditations, would find the poor, simple Brother sitting under the shade of the pear-tree, close to the bee-hives, rocking the little baby in his arms, singing strange, crazy songs to it, and gazing far away into the blue, empty sky with his curious, pale eyes.

Although, as Otto grew up into boyhood, his lessons and his tasks separated him from Brother John, the bond between them seemed to grow stronger rather than weaker. During the hours that Otto had for his own they were scarcely ever apart. Down in the vineyard, where the monks were gathering the grapes for the vintage, in the garden, or in the fields, the two were always seen together, either wandering hand in hand, or seated in some shady nook or corner.

But most of all they loved to lie up in the airy wooden belfry; the great gaping bell hanging darkly above them, the mouldering cross-beams glimmering far up under the dim shadows of the roof, where dwelt a great brown owl that, unfrightened at their familiar presence, stared down at them with his round, solemn eyes. Below them stretched the white walls of the garden, beyond them the vineyard, and beyond that again the far shining river, that seemed to Otto's mind to lead into wonder-land. There the two would lie upon the belfry floor by the hour, talking together of the strangest things.

"I saw the dear Angel Gabriel again yester morn," said Brother John.

"So!" says Otto, seriously; "and where was that?"

"It was out in the garden, in the old apple-tree," said Brother John. "I was walking there, and my wits were running around in the grass like a mouse. What heard I but a wonderful sound of singing, and it was like the hum of a great bee, only sweeter than honey. So I looked up into the tree, and there I saw two sparks. I thought at first that they were two stars that had fallen out of heaven; but what think you they were, little child?"

"I do not know," said Otto, breathlessly.

"They were angel's eyes," said Brother John; and he smiled in the strangest way, as he gazed up into the blue sky. "So I looked at the two sparks and felt happy, as one does in spring time when the cold weather is gone, and the warm sun shines, and the cuckoo sings again. Then, by-and-by, I saw the face to which the eyes belonged. First, it shone white and thin like the moon in the

THE POOR, SIMPLE BROTHER SITTING UNDER THE PEAR-TREE, CLOSE TO THE BEE-HIVES, ROCKING THE LITTLE BABY IN HIS ARMS.

daylight; but it grew brighter and brighter, until it hurt one's eyes to look at it, as though it had been the blessed sun itself. Angel Gabriel's hand was as white as silver, and in it he held a green bough with blossoms, like those that grow on the thorn bush. As for his robe, it was all of one piece, and finer than the Father Abbot's linen, and shone beside like the sunlight on pure snow. So I knew from all these things that it was the blessed Angel Gabriel."

"What do they say about this tree, Brother John?" said he to me.

"They say it is dying, my Lord Angel," said I, "and that the gardener will bring a sharp axe and cut it down."

"'And what dost thou say about it, Brother John?' said he."

"'I also say yes, and that it is dying,' said I."

"At that he smiled until his face shone so bright that I had to shut my eyes."

"'Now I begin to believe, Brother John, that thou art as foolish as men say,' said he. 'Look, till I show thee.' And thereat I opened mine eyes again."

"Then Angel Gabriel touched the dead branches with the flowery twig that he held in his hand, and there was the dead wood all covered with green leaves, and fair blossoms and beautiful apples as yellow as gold. Each smelling more sweetly than a garden of flowers, and better to the taste than white bread and honey.

"'They are souls of the apples,' said the good Angel,' and they can never wither and die.'

"'Then I'll tell the gardener that he shall not cut the tree down,' said I."

"'No, no,' said the dear Gabriel, 'that will never do, for if the tree is not cut down here on the earth, it can never be planted in paradise.'

Here Brother John stopped short in his story, and began singing one of his crazy songs, as he gazed with his pale eyes far away into nothing at all.

"But tell me, Brother John," said little Otto, in a hushed voice, "what else did the good Angel say to thee?"

Brother John stopped short in his song and began looking from right to left, and up and down, as though to gather his wits.

"So!" said he, "there was something else that he told me. Tschk! If I could but think now. Yes, good! This is it - *'Nothing that has lived,' said he, 'shall ever die, and nothing that has died shall ever live.'*

Otto drew a deep breath. "I would that I might see the beautiful Angel Gabriel sometime," said he; but Brother John was singing again and did not seem to hear what he said.

Next to Brother John, the nearest one to the little child was the good Abbot Otto, for though he had never seen wonderful things with the eyes of his soul, such as Brother John's had beheld, and so could not tell of them, he was yet able to give little Otto another pleasure that no one else could give.

He was a great lover of books, the old Abbot, and had under lock and key wonderful and beautiful volumes, bound in hog-skin and metal, and with covers inlaid with carved ivory, or studded with precious stones. But within these covers, beautiful as they were, lay the real wonder of the books, like the soul in the body; for there, beside the black letters and initials, gay with red and blue and gold, were beautiful pictures painted upon the creamy parchment. Saints and Angels, the Blessed Virgin with the golden oriole about her head, good St. Joseph, the three Kings; the simple Shepherds kneeling in the fields, while Angels with glories about their brow called to the poor Peasants from the blue sky above. But, most beautiful of all was the picture of the Christ Child lying in the manger, with the mild-eyed Kine gazing at him.

Sometimes the old Abbot would unlock the iron-bound chest where these treasures lay hidden, and carefully and lovingly brushing the few grains of dust from them, would lay them upon the table beside the oriel window in front of his little namesake, allowing the little boy freedom to turn the leaves as he chose.

Always it was one picture that little Otto sought; the Christ Child in the manger, with the Virgin, St. Joseph, the Shepherds, and the Kine. And as he would hang breathlessly gazing and gazing upon it, the old Abbot would sit watching him with a faint, half-sad smile flickering around his thin lips and his pale, narrow face.

It was a pleasant, peaceful life, but by-and-by the end came.

Otto was now nearly twelve years old.

One bright, clear day, near the hour of noon, little Otto heard the porter's bell sounding below in the court-yard - dong! dong! Brother Emmanuel had been appointed as the boy's instructor, and just then Otto was conning his lessons in the good monk's cell. Nevertheless, at the sound of the bell he pricked up his ears and listened, for a visitor was a strange matter in that out-of- the-way place, and he wondered who it could be. So, while his wits wandered his lessons lagged.

"Postera Phoeba lustrabat lampade terras," continued Brother Emmanuel, inexorably running his horny finger-nail beneath the line, "humentemque Aurora polo dimoverat umbram -" the lesson dragged along.

Just then a sandaled footstep sounded without, in the stone corridor, and a light tap fell upon Brother Emmanuel's door. It was Brother Ignatius, and the Abbot wished little Otto to come to the refectory.

As they crossed the court-yard Otto stared to see a group of mail-clad men-at-arms, some sitting upon their horses, some standing by the saddle-bow. "Yonder is the young baron," he heard one of them say in a gruff voice, and thereupon all turned and stared at him.

A stranger was in the refectory, standing beside the good old Abbot, while food and wine were being brought and set upon the table for his refreshment; a great, tall, broad-shouldered man, beside whom the Abbot looked thinner and slighter than ever.

The stranger was clad all in polished and gleaming armor, of plate and chain, over which was drawn a loose robe of gray woollen stuff, reaching to

ALWAYS IT WAS ONE PICTURE THAT LITTLE OTTO SOUGHT.

the knees and bound about the waist by a broad leathern sword-belt. Upon his arm he carried a great helmet which he had just removed from his head. His face was weather-beaten and rugged, and on lip and chin was a wiry, bristling beard; once red, now frosted with white.

Brother Ignatius had bidden Otto to enter, and had then closed the door behind him; and now, as the lad walked slowly up the long room, he gazed with round, wondering blue eyes at the stranger.

"Dost know who I am, Otto ? said the mail-clad knight, in a deep, growling voice.

"Methinks you are my father, sir," said Otto.

"Aye, thou art right," said Baron Conrad, "and I am glad to see that these milk-churning monks have not allowed thee to forget me, and who thou art thyself."

"An' it please you," said Otto, "no one churneth milk here but Brother Fritz; we be makers of wine and not makers of butter, at St. Michaelsburg."

Baron Conrad broke into a great, loud laugh, but Abbot Otto's sad and thoughtful face lit up with no shadow of an answering smile.

"Conrad," said he, turning to the other, "again let me urge thee; do not take the child hence, his life can never be your life, for he is not fitted for it. I had thought," said he, after a moment's pause, "I had thought that thou hadst meant to consecrate him - this motherless one - to the care of the Universal Mother Church."

"So!" said the Baron, "thou hadst thought that, hadst thou? Thou hadst thought that I had intended to deliver over this boy, the last of the Vuelphs, to the arms of the Church? What then was to become of our name and the glory of our race if it was to end with him in a monastery? No, Drachenhausen is the home of the Vuelphs, and there the last of the race shall live as his sires have lived before him, holding to his rights by the power and the might of his right hand."

The Abbot turned and looked at the boy, who was gaping in simple wide-eyed wonderment from one to the other as they spoke.

"And dost thou think, Conrad," said the old man, in his gentle, patient voice, "that that poor child can maintain his rights by the strength of his right hand?"

The Baron's look followed the Abbot's, and he said nothing.

In the few seconds of silence that followed, little Otto, in his simple mind, was wondering what all this talk portended. Why had his father come hither to St. Michaelsburg, lighting up the dim silence of the monastery with the flash and ring of his polished armor? Why had he talked about churning butter but now, when all the world knew that the monks of St. Michaelsburg made wine.

It was Baron Conrad's deep voice that broke the little pause of silence.

"If you have made a milkmaid of the boy," he burst out at last, "I thank the dear heaven that there is yet time to undo your work and to make a man of him."

The Abbot sighed. "The child is yours, Conrad," said he, "the will of the blessed saints be done. Mayhap if he goes to dwell at Drachenhausen he may make you the better instead of you making him the worse."

Then light came to the darkness of little Otto's wonderment; he saw what all this talk meant and why his father had come hither. He was to leave the happy, sunny silence of the dear White Cross, and to go out into that great world that he had so often looked down upon from the high windy belfry on the steep hillside.

Chapter - VI

How Otto Lived in the Dragon's House

The gates of the Monastery stood wide open, the world lay beyond, and all was ready for departure. Baron Conrad and his men-at-arms sat foot in stirrup, the milk-white horse that had been brought for Otto stood waiting for him beside his father's great charger.

"Farewell, Otto," said the good old Abbot, as he stooped and kissed the boy's cheek.

"Farewell," answered Otto, in his simple, quiet way, and it brought a pang to the old man's heart that the child should seem to grieve so little at the leave-taking.

"Farewell, Otto," said the brethren that stood about, "farewell, farewell."

Then poor brother John came forward and took the boy's hand, and looked up into his face as he sat upon his horse. "We will meet again," said he, with his strange, vacant smile, "but maybe it will be in Paradise, and there perhaps they will let us lie in the father's belfry, and look down upon the angels in the court- yard below."

"Aye," answered Otto, with an answering smile.

"Forward," cried the Baron, in a deep voice, and with a clash of hoofs and jingle of armor they were gone, and the great wooden gates were shut to behind them.

Down the steep winding pathway they rode, and out into the great wide world beyond, upon which Otto and brother John had gazed so often from the wooden belfry of the White Cross on the hill.

"Hast been taught to ride a horse by the priests up yonder on Michaelsburg?" asked the Baron, when they had reached the level road.

POOR BROTHER JOHN CAME FORWARD AND TOOK THE BOY'S HAND.

"Nay," said Otto; "we had no horse to ride, but only to bring in the harvest or the grapes from the further vineyards to the vintage."

"Prut," said the Baron, "methought the abbot would have had enough of the blood of old days in his veins to have taught thee what is fitting for a knight to know; art not afeared?"

"Nay," said Otto, with a smile, "I am not afeared."

"There at least thou showest thyself a Vuelph," said the grim Baron. But perhaps Otto's thought of fear and Baron Conrad's thought of fear were two very different matters.

The afternoon had passed by the time they had reached the end of their journey. Up the steep, stony path they rode to the drawbridge and the great gaping gateway of Drachenhausen, where wall and tower and battlement looked darker and more forbidding than ever in the gray twilight of the coming night. Little Otto looked up with great, wondering, awe-struck eyes at this grim new home of his.

The next moment they clattered over the drawbridge that spanned the narrow black gulph between the roadway and the wall, and the next were past the echoing arch of the great gateway and in the gray gloaming of the paved court-yard within.

Otto looked around upon the many faces gathered there to catch the first sight of the little baron; hard, rugged faces, seamed and weather-beaten; very different from those of the gentle brethren among whom he had lived, and it seemed strange to him that there was none there whom he should know.

As he climbed the steep, stony steps to the door of the Baron's house, old Ursela came running down to meet him. She flung her withered arms around him and hugged him close to her. "My little child," she cried, and then fell to sobbing as though her heart would break.

"Here is someone knoweth me," thought the little boy.

His new home was all very strange and wonderful to Otto; the armors, the trophies, the flags, the long galleries with their ranges of rooms, the great hall below with its vaulted roof and its great fireplace of grotesquely carved stone, and all the strange people with their lives and thoughts so different from what he had been used to know.

And it was a wonderful thing to explore all the strange places in the dark old castle; places where it seemed to Otto no one could have ever been before.

Once he wandered down a long, dark passageway below the hall, pushed open a narrow, iron-bound oaken door, and found himself all at once in a strange new land; the gray light, coming in through a range of tall, narrow windows, fell upon a row of silent, motionless figures carven in stone, knights and ladies in strange armor and dress; each lying upon his or her stony couch with clasped hands, and gazing with fixed, motionless, stony eyeballs up into the gloomy, vaulted arch above them. There lay, in a cold, silent row, all of the Vuelphs who had died since the ancient castle had been built.

It was the chapel into which Otto had made his way, now long since fallen out of use excepting as a burial place of the race.

At another time he clambered up into the loft under the high peaked roof, where lay numberless forgotten things covered with the dim dust of years. There a flock of pigeons had made their roost, and flapped noisily out into the sunlight when he pushed open the door from below. Here he hunted among the mouldering things of the past until, oh, joy of joys! in an ancient oaken chest he found a great lot of worm-eaten books, that had belonged to some old chaplain of the castle in days gone by. They were not precious and beautiful volumes, such as the Father Abbot had showed him, but all the same they had their quaint painted pictures of the blessed saints and angels.

Again, at another time, going into the court-yard, Otto had found the door of Melchior's tower standing invitingly open, for old Hilda, Schwartz Carl's wife, had come down below upon some business or other.

Then upon the shaky wooden steps Otto ran without waiting for a second thought, for he had often gazed at those curious buildings hanging so far up in the air, and had wondered what they were like. Round and round and up and up Otto climbed, until his head spun. At last he reached a landing-stage, and gazing over the edge and down, beheld the stone pavement far, far below, lit by a faint glimmer of light that entered through the arched doorway. Otto clutched tight hold of the wooden rail, he had no thought that he had climbed so far.

Upon the other side of the landing was a window that pierced the thick stone walls of the tower; out of the window he looked, and then drew suddenly back again with a gasp, for it was through the outer wall he peered, and down, down below in the dizzy depths he saw the hard gray rocks, where the black swine, looking no larger than ants in the distance, fed upon the refuse thrown out over the walls of the castle. There lay the moving tree-tops like a billowy green sea, and the coarse thatched roofs of the peasant cottages, round which crawled the little children like tiny human specks.

Then Otto turned and crept down the stairs, frightened at the height to which he had climbed.

At the doorway he met Mother Hilda. "Bless us," she cried, starting back and crossing herself, and then, seeing who it was, ducked him a courtesy with as pleasant a smile as her forbidding face, with its little deep-set eyes, was able to put upon itself.

Old Ursela seemed nearer to the boy than anyone else about the castle, excepting it was his father, and it was a newfound delight to Otto to sit beside her and listen to her quaint stories, so different from the monkish tales that he had heard and read at the monastery.

But one day it was a tale of a different sort that she told him, and one that opened his eyes to what he had never dreamed of before.

The mellow sunlight fell through the window upon old Ursela, as she sat in the warmth with her distaff in her hands while Otto lay close to her feet upon a bear skin, silently thinking over the strange story of a brave knight and a fiery dragon that she had just told him. Suddenly Ursela broke the silence.

OTTO LAY CLOSE TO HER FEET UPON A BEAR SKIN.

"Little one," said she, "thou art wondrously like thy own dear mother; didst ever hear how she died?"

"Nay," said Otto, "but tell me, Ursela, how it was."

"Tis strange," said the old woman, "that no one should have told thee in all this time." And then, in her own fashion she related to him the story of how his father had set forth upon that expedition in spite of all that Otto's mother had said, beseeching him to abide at home; how he had been foully wounded, and how the poor lady had died from her fright and grief.

Otto listened with eyes that grew wider and wider, though not all with wonder; he no longer lay upon the bear skin, but sat up with his hands clasped. For a moment or two after the old woman had ended her story, he sat staring silently at her. Then he cried out, in a sharp voice, "And is this truth that you tell me, Ursela? and did my father seek to rob the towns people of their goods?"

Old Ursela laughed. "Aye," said she, "that he did and many times. Ah! me, those day's are all gone now." And she fetched a deep sigh. "Then we lived in plenty and had both silks and linens and velvets besides in the store closets and were able to buy good wines and live in plenty upon the best. Now we dress in frieze and live upon what we can get and sometimes that is little enough, with nothing better than sour beer to drink. But there is one comfort in it all, and that is that our good Baron paid back the score he owed the Trutz-Drachen people not only for that, but for all that they had done from the very first."

Thereupon she went on to tell Otto how Baron Conrad had fulfilled the pledge of revenge that he had made Abbot Otto, how he had watched day after day until one time he had caught the Trutz-Drachen folk, with Baron Frederick at their head, in a narrow defile back of the Kaiserburg; of the fierce fight that was there fought; of how the Roderburgs at last fled, leaving Baron Frederick behind them wounded; of how he had kneeled before the Baron Conrad, asking for mercy, and of how Baron Conrad had answered, "Aye, thou shalt have such mercy as thou deservest," and had therewith raised his great two-handed sword and laid his kneeling enemy dead at one blow.

Poor little Otto had never dreamed that such cruelty and wickedness could be. He listened to the old woman's story with gaping horror, and when the last came and she told him, with a smack of her lips, how his father had killed his enemy with his own hand, he gave a gasping cry and sprang to his feet. Just then the door at the other end of the chamber was noisily opened, and Baron Conrad himself strode into the room. Otto turned his head, and seeing who it was, gave another cry, loud and quavering, and ran to his father and caught him by the hand.

"Oh, father!" he cried, "oh, father! Is it true that thou hast killed a man with thy own hand?"

"Aye," said the Baron, grimly, "it is true enough, and I think me I have killed many more than one. But what of that, Otto? Thou must get out of those foolish notions that the old monks have taught thee. Here in the world it is different from what it is at St. Michaelsburg; here a man must either slay or be slain."

But poor little Otto, with his face hidden in his father's robe, cried as though his heart would break. "Oh, father!" he said, again and again, "it cannot be - it cannot be that thou who art so kind to me should have killed a man with thine own hands." Then: "I wish that I were back in the monastery again; I am afraid out here in the great wide world; perhaps somebody may kill me, for I am only a weak little boy and could not save my own life if they chose to take it from me."

Baron Conrad looked down upon Otto all this while, drawing his bushy eyebrows together. Once he reached out his hand as though to stroke the boy's hair, but drew it back again.

Turning angrily upon the old woman, "Ursela," said he, "thou must tell the child no more such stories as these; he knowest not at all of such things as yet. Keep thy tongue busy with the old woman's tales that he loves to hear thee tell, and leave it with me to teach him what becometh a true knight and a Vuelph."

That night the father and son sat together beside the roaring fire in the great ball. "Tell me, Otto," said the Baron, "dost thou hate me for having done what Ursela told thee today that I did?"

Otto looked for a while into his father's face. "I know not," said he at last, in his quaint, quiet voice, "but methinks that I do not hate thee for it."

The Baron drew his bushy brows together until his eyes twinkled out of the depths beneath them, then of a sudden he broke into a great loud laugh, smiting his horny palm with a smack upon his thigh.

SLOWLY RAISING HIMSELF UPON THE NARROW FOOTHOLD HE PEEPED CAUTIOUSLY WITHIN.

Chapter - VII

The Red Cock Crows on Drachenhausen

There was a new emperor in Germany who had come from a far away Swiss castle; Count Rudolph of Hapsburg, a good, honest man with a good, honest, homely face, but bringing with him a stern sense of justice and of right, and a determination to put down the lawlessness of the savage German barons among whom he had come as Emperor.

One day two strangers came galloping up the winding path to the gates of the Dragon's house. A horn sounded thin and clear, a parley was held across the chasm in the road between the two strangers and the porter who appeared at the little wicket. Then a messenger was sent running to the Baron, who presently came striding across the open court-yard to the gateway to parley with the strangers.

The two bore with them a folded parchment with a great red seal hanging from it like a clot of blood; it was a message from the Emperor demanding that the Baron should come to the Imperial Court to answer certain charges that had been brought against him, and to give his bond to maintain the peace of the empire.

One by one those barons who had been carrying on their private wars, or had been despoiling the burgher folk in their traffic from town to town, and against whom complaint had been lodged, were summoned to the Imperial Court, where they were compelled to promise peace and to swear allegiance to the new order of things. All those who came willingly were allowed to return home again after giving security for maintaining the peace; all those who came not willingly were either brought in chains or rooted out of their strongholds with fire and sword, and their roofs burned over their heads.

Now it was Baron Conrad's turn to be summoned to the Imperial Court, for complaint had been lodged against him by his old enemy of Trutz-Drachen - Baron Henry - the nephew of the old Baron Frederick who had been slain while kneeling in the dust of the road back of the Kaiserburg.

THE GRIM BARON SAT SILENT WITH HIS CHIN RESTING UPON HIS CLENCHED FIST.

No one at Drachenhausen could read but Master Rudolph, the steward, who was sand blind, and little Otto. So the boy read the summons to his father, while the grim Baron sat silent with his chin resting upon his clenched fist and his eyebrows drawn together into a thoughtful frown as he gazed into the pale face of his son, who sat by the rude oaken table with the great parchment spread out before him.

Should he answer the summons, or scorn it as he would have done under the old emperors? Baron Conrad knew not which to do; pride said one thing and policy another. The Emperor was a man with an iron hand, and Baron Conrad knew what had happened to those who had refused to obey the imperial commands. So at last he decided that he would go to the court, taking with him a suitable escort to support his dignity.

It was with nearly a hundred armed men clattering behind him that Baron Conrad rode away to court to answer the imperial summons. The castle was stripped of its fighting men, and only eight remained behind to guard the great stone fortress and the little simple-witted boy.

It was a sad mistake.

Three days had passed since the Baron had left the castle, and now the third night had come. The moon was hanging midway in the sky, white and full, for it was barely past midnight.

The high precipitous banks of the rocky road threw a dense black shadow into the gully below, and in that crooked inky line that scarred the white face of the moonlit rocks a band of some thirty men were creeping slowly and stealthily nearer and nearer to Castle Drachenhausen. At the head of them was a tall, slender knight clad in light chain armor, his head covered only by a steel cap or bascinet.

Along the shadow they crept, with only now and then a faint clink or jingle of armor to break the stillness, for most of those who followed the armed knight were clad in leathern jerkins; only one or two wearing even so much as a steel breast-plate by way of armor.

So at last they reached the chasm that yawned beneath the roadway, and there they stopped, for they had reached the spot toward which they had been journeying. It was Baron Henry of Trutz-Drachen who had thus come in the silence of the night time to the Dragon's house, and his visit boded no good to those within.

The Baron and two or three of his men talked together in low tones, now and then looking up at the sheer wall that towered above them.

"Yonder is the place, Lord Baron," said one of those who stood with him. "I have scanned every foot of the wall at night for a week past. An we get not in by that way, we get not in at all. A keen eye, a true aim, and a bold man are all that we need, and the business is done." Here again all looked upward at the gray wall above them, rising up in the silent night air.

High aloft hung the wooden bartizan or watch-tower, clinging to the face of the outer wall and looming black against the pale sky above. Three great beams pierced the wall, and upon them the wooden tower rested. The middle beam jutted out beyond the rest to the distance of five or six feet, and the end of it was carved into the rude semblance of a dragon's head.

"So, good," said the Baron at last; "then let us see if thy plan holds, and if Hans Schmidt's aim is true enough to earn the three marks that I have promised him. Where is the bag?"

One of those who stood near handed the Baron a leathern pouch, the Baron opened it and drew out a ball of fine thread, another of twine, a coil of stout rope, and a great bundle that looked, until it was unrolled, like a coarse fish-net. It was a rope ladder. While these were being made ready, Hans Schmidt, a thick-set, low-browed, broad-shouldered archer, strung his stout bow, and carefully choosing three arrows from those in his quiver, he stuck them point downward in the earth. Unwinding the ball of thread, he laid it loosely in large loops upon the ground so that it might run easily without hitching, then he tied the end of the thread tightly around one of his arrows. He fitted the arrow to the bow and drew the feather to his ear. Twang! rang the bowstring, and the feathered messenger flew whistling upon its errand to the watch-tower. The very first shaft did the work.

"Good," said Hans Schmidt, the archer, in his heavy voice, "the three marks are mine, Lord Baron."

The arrow had fallen over and across the jutting beam between the carved dragon's head and the bartizan, carrying with it the thread, which now hung from above, glimmering white in the moonlight like a cobweb.

The rest was an easy task enough. First the twine was drawn up to and over the beam by the thread, then the rope was drawn up by the twine, and last of all the rope ladder by the rope. There it hung like a thin, slender black line against the silent gray walls.

"And now," said the Baron, "who will go first and win fifty marks for his own, and climb the rope ladder to the tower yonder?" Those around hesitated. "Is there none brave enough to venture?" said the Baron, after a pause of silence.

A stout, young fellow, of about eighteen years of age, stepped forward and flung his flat leathern cap upon the ground. "I will go, my Lord Baron," said he.

"Good," said the Baron, "the fifty marks are thine. And now listen, if thou findest no one in the watch-tower, whistle thus; if the watchman be at his post, see that thou makest all safe before thou givest the signal. When all is ready the others will follow thee. And now go and good luck go with thee."

The young fellow spat upon his hands and, seizing the ropes, began slowly and carefully to mount the flimsy, shaking ladder. Those below held it as tight as they were able, but nevertheless he swung backward and forward and round and round as he climbed steadily upward. Once he stopped upon the way, and those below saw him clutch the ladder close to him as though dizzied by the height and the motion but he soon began again, up, up, up like some great black spider. Presently he came out from the black shadow below and into the white moonlight, and then his shadow followed him step by step up the gray

SLOWLY RAISING HIMSELF UPON THE NARROW FOOTHOLD HE PEEPED CAUTIOUSLY WITHIN.

wall upon his way. At last he reached the jutting beam, and there again he stopped for a moment clutching tightly to it. The next he was upon the beam, dragging himself toward the window of the bartizan just above. Slowly raising himself upon his narrow foothold he peeped cautiously within. Those watching him from be low saw him slip his hand softly to his side, and then place something between his teeth. It was his dagger. Reaching up, he clutched the window sill above him and, with a silent spring, seated himself upon it. The next moment he disappeared within. A few seconds of silence followed, then of sudden a sharp gurgling cry broke the stillness. There was another pause of silence, then a faint shrill whistle sounded from above.

"Who will go next?" said the Baron. It was Hans Schmidt who stepped forward. Another followed the arch up the ladder, and another, and another. Last of all went the Baron Henry himself, and nothing was left but the rope ladder hanging from above, and swaying back and forth in the wind.

That night Schwartz Carl had been bousing it over a pot of yellow wine in the pantry with his old crony, Master Rudolph, the steward; and the two, chatting and gossiping together, had passed the time away until long after the rest of the castle had been wrapped in sleep. Then, perhaps a little unsteady upon his feet, Schwartz Carl betook himself homeward to the Melchior tower.

He stood for a while in the shadow of the doorway, gazing up into the pale sky above him at the great, bright, round moon, that hung like a bubble above the sharp peaks of the roofs standing black as ink against the sky. But all of a sudden he started up from the post against which he had been leaning, and with head bent to one side, stood listening breathlessly, for he too had heard that smothered cry from the watch-tower. So he stood intently, motionlessly, listening, listening; but all was silent except for the monotonous dripping of water in one of the nooks of the court-yard, and the distant murmur of the river borne upon the breath of the night air. "Mayhap I was mistaken," muttered Schwartz Carl to himself.

But the next moment the silence was broken again by a faint, shrill whistle; what did it mean?

Back of the heavy oaken door of the tower was Schwartz Carl's cross-bow, the portable windlass with which the bowstring was drawn back, and a pouch of bolts. Schwartz Carl reached back into the darkness, fumbling in the gloom until his fingers met the weapon. Setting his foot in the iron stirrup at the end of the stock, he wound the stout bow-string into the notch of the trigger, and carefully fitted the heavy, murderous-looking bolt into the groove.

Minute after minute passed, and Schwartz Carl, holding his arbelast in his hand, stood silently waiting and watching in the sharp-cut, black shadow of the doorway, motionless as a stone statue. Minute after minute passed. Suddenly there was a movement in the shadow of the arch of the great gateway

SCHWARTZ CARL, HOLDING HIS ARBELAST IN HIS HAND, STOOD SILENTLY WATCHING

across the court-yard, and the next moment a leathern-clad figure crept noiselessly out upon the moonlit pavement, and stood there listening, his head bent to one side. Schwartz Carl knew very well that it was no one belonging to the castle, and, from the nature of his action, that he was upon no good errand.

He did not stop to challenge the suspicious stranger. The taking of another's life was thought too small a matter for much thought or care in those days. Schwartz Carl would have shot a man for a much smaller reason than the suspicious actions of this fellow. The leather-clad figure stood a fine target in the moonlight for a cross-bow bolt. Schwartz Carl slowly raised the weapon to his shoulder and took a long and steady aim. Just then the stranger put his fingers to his lips and gave a low, shrill whistle. It was the last whistle that he was to give upon this earth. There was a sharp, jarring twang of the bow-string, the hiss of the flying bolt, and the dull thud as it struck its mark. The man gave a shrill, quavering cry, and went staggering back, and then fell all of a heap against the wall behind him. As though in answer to the cry, half a dozen men rushed tumultuously out from the shadow of the gateway whence the stranger had just come, and then stood in the court-yard, looking uncertainly this way and that, not knowing from what quarter the stroke had come that had laid their comrade low.

But Schwartz Carl did not give them time to discover that; there was no chance to string his cumbersome weapon again; down he flung it upon the ground. "To arms!" he roared in a voice of thunder, and then clapped to the door of Melchior's tower and shot the great iron bolts with a clang and rattle.

The next instant the Trutz-Drachen men were thundering at the door, but Schwartz Carl was already far up the winding steps.

But now the others came pouring out from the gateway. "To the house," roared Baron Henry.

Then suddenly a clashing, clanging uproar crashed out upon the night. Dong! Dong! It was the great alarm bell from Melchior's tower - Schwartz Carl was at his post.

Little Baron Otto lay sleeping upon the great rough bed in his room, dreaming of the White Cross on the hill and of brother John. By and by he heard the convent bell ringing, and knew that there must be visitors at the gate, for loud voices sounded through his dream. Presently he knew that he was coming awake, but though the sunny monastery garden grew dimmer and dimmer to his sleeping sight, the clanging of the bell and the sound of shouts grew louder and louder. Then he opened his eyes. Flaming red lights from torches, carried hither and thither by people in the court-yard outside, flashed and ran along the wall of his room. Hoarse shouts and cries filled the air, and suddenly the shrill, piercing shriek of a woman rang from wall to wall; and through the noises the great bell from far above upon Melchior's tower clashed and clanged its harsh, resonant alarm.

Otto sprang from his bed and looked out of the window and down upon the court-yard below. "Dear God! what dreadful thing hath happened?" he cried and clasped his hands together.

A cloud of smoke was pouring out from the windows of the building across the court-yard, whence a dull ruddy glow flashed and flickered. Strange men were running here and there with flaming torches, and the now continuous shrieking of women pierced the air.

Just beneath the window lay the figure of a man half naked and face downward upon the stones. Then suddenly Otto cried out in fear and horror, for, as he looked with dazed and bewildered eyes down into the lurid court-yard beneath, a savage man, in a shining breast-plate and steel cap, came dragging the dark, silent figure of a woman across the stones; but whether she was dead or in a swoon, Otto could not tell.

And every moment the pulsing of that dull red glare from the windows of the building across the court-yard shone more brightly, and the glare from other flaming buildings, which Otto could not see from his window, turned the black, starry night into a lurid day.

Just then the door of the room was burst open, and in rushed poor old Ursela, crazy with her terror. She flung herself down upon the floor and caught Otto around the knees. "Save me!" she cried, "save me!" as though the poor, pale child could be of any help to her at such a time. In the passageway without shone the light of torches, and the sound of loud footsteps came nearer and nearer.

And still through all the din sounded continually the clash and clang and clamor of the great alarm bell.

The red light flashed into the room, and in the doorway stood a tall, thin figure clad from head to foot in glittering chain armor. From behind this fierce knight, with his dark, narrow, cruel face, its deep-set eyes glistening in the light of the torches, crowded six or eight savage, low-browed, brutal men, who stared into the room and at the white-faced boy as he stood by the window with the old woman clinging to his knees and praying to him for help.

"We have cracked the nut and here is the kernel," said one of them who stood behind the rest, and thereupon a roar of brutal laughter went up. But the cruel face of the armed knight never relaxed into a smile; he strode into the room and laid his iron hand heavily upon the boy's shoulder. "Art thou the young Baron Otto?" said he, in a harsh voice.

"Aye," said the lad; "but do not kill me."

The knight did not answer him. "Fetch the cord hither," said he, "and drag the old witch away."

It took two of them to loosen poor old Ursela's crazy clutch from about her young master. Then amid roars of laughter they dragged her away, screaming and scratching and striking with her fists.

They drew back Otto's arms behind his back and wrapped them round and round with a bowstring. Then they pushed and hustled and thrust him

HE STRODE FORWARD INTO THE ROOM AND LAID HIS HAND HEAVILY ON THE BOY'S SHOULDER.

forth from the room and along the passageway, now bright with the flames that roared and crackled without. Down the steep stairway they drove him, where thrice he stumbled and fell amid roars of laughter. At last they were out into the open air of the court-yard. Here was a terrible sight, but Otto saw nothing of it; his blue eyes were gazing far away, and his lips moved softly with the prayer that the good monks of St. Michaelsburg had taught him, for he thought that they meant to slay him.

All around the court-yard the flames roared and snapped and crackled. Four or five figures lay scattered here and there, silent in all the glare and uproar. The heat was so intense that they were soon forced back into the shelter of the great gateway, where the women captives, under the guard of three or four of the Trutz-Drachen men, were crowded together in dumb, bewildered terror. Only one man was to be seen among the captives, poor, old, half blind Master Rudolph, the steward, who crouched tremblingly among the women. They had set the blaze to Melchior's tower, and now, below, it was a seething furnace. Above, the smoke rolled in black clouds from the windows, but still the alarm bell sounded through all the blaze and smoke. Higher and higher the flames rose; a trickle of fire ran along the frame buildings hanging aloft in the air. A clear flame burst out at the peak of the roof, but still the bell rang forth its clamorous clangor. Presently those who watched below saw the cluster of buildings bend and sink and sway; there was a crash and roar, a cloud of sparks flew up as though to the very heavens themselves, and the bell of Melchior's tower was stilled forever. A great shout arose from the watching, upturned faces.

"Forward!" cried Baron Henry, and out from the gateway they swept and across the drawbridge, leaving Drachenhausen behind them a flaming furnace blazing against the gray of the early dawning.

Chapter - VIII

In the House of the Dragon Scorner

Tall, narrow, gloomy room; no furniture but a rude bench a bare stone floor, cold stone walls and a gloomy ceiling of arched stone over head; a long, narrow slit of a window high above in the wall, through the iron bars of which Otto could see a small patch of blue sky and now and then a darting swallow, for an instant seen, the next instant gone. Such was the little baron's prison in Trutz-Drachen. Fastened to a bolt and hanging against the walls, hung a pair of heavy chains with gaping fetters at the ends. They were thick with rust, and the red stain of the rust streaked the wall below where they hung like a smear of blood. Little Otto shuddered as he looked at them; can those be meant for me, he thought.

Nothing was to be seen but that one patch of blue sky far up in the wall. No sound from without was to be heard in that gloomy cell of stone, for the window pierced the outer wall, and the earth and its noises lay far below.

Suddenly a door crashed without, and the footsteps of men were heard coming along the corridor. They stopped in front of Otto's cell; he heard the jingle of keys, and then a loud rattle of one thrust into the lock of the heavy oaken door. The rusty bolt was shot back with a screech, the door opened, and there stood Baron Henry, no longer in his armor, but clad in a long black robe that reached nearly to his feet, a broad leather belt was girdled about his waist, and from it dangled a short, heavy hunting sword.

Another man was with the Baron, a heavy-faced fellow clad in a leathern jerkin over which was drawn a short coat of linked mail.

The two stood for a moment looking into the room, and Otto, his pale face glimmering in the gloom, sat upon the edge of the heavy wooden bench

"THEN DOST THOU NOT KNOW WHY I AM HERE?" SAID THE BARON.

or bed, looking back at them out of his great blue eyes. Then the two entered and closed the door behind them.

"Dost thou know why thou art here?" said the Baron, in his deep, harsh voice.

"Nay," said Otto, "I know not."

"So?" said the Baron. "Then I will tell thee. Three years ago the good Baron Frederick, my uncle, kneeled in the dust and besought mercy at thy father's hands; the mercy he received was the coward blow that slew him. Thou knowest the story?"

"Aye," said Otto, tremblingly, "I know it."

"Then dost thou not know why I am here?" said the Baron.

"Nay, dear Lord Baron, I know not," said poor little Otto, and began to weep.

The Baron stood for a moment or two looking gloomily upon him, as the little boy sat there with the tears running down his white face.

"I will tell thee," said he, at last; "I swore an oath that the red cock should crow on Drachenhausen, and I have given it to the dames. I swore an oath that no Vuelph that ever left my hands should be able to strike such a blow as thy father gave to Baron Frederick, and now I will fulfil that too. Catch the boy, Casper, and hold him."

As the man in the mail shirt stepped toward little Otto, the boy leaped up from where he sat and caught the Baron about the knees. "Oh! dear Lord Baron," he cried, "do not harm me; I am only a little child, I have never done harm to thee; do not harm me."

"Take him away," said the Baron, harshly.

The fellow stooped, and loosening Otto's hold, in spite of his struggles and cries, carried him to the bench, against which he held him, whilst the Baron stood above him.

Baron Henry and the other came forth from the cell, carefully closing the wooden door behind them. At the end of the corridor the Baron turned, "Let the leech be sent to the boy," said he. And then he turned and walked away.

Otto lay upon the hard couch in his cell, covered with a shaggy bear skin. His face was paler and thinner than ever, and dark rings encircled his blue eyes. He was looking toward the door, for there was a noise of someone fumbling with the lock without.

Since that dreadful day when Baron Henry had come to his cell, only two souls had visited Otto. One was the fellow who had come with the Baron that time; his name, Otto found, was Casper. He brought the boy his rude meals of bread and meat and water. The other visitor was the leech or doctor, a thin, weasand little man, with a kindly, wrinkled face and a gossiping tongue, who, besides binding wounds, bleeding, and leeching, and administering his simple remedies to those who were taken sick in the castle, acted as the Baron's barber.

The Baron had left the key in the lock of the door, so that these two might enter when they chose, but Otto knew that it was neither the one nor the other whom he now heard at the door, working uncertainly with the key, striving to turn it in the rusty, cumbersome lock. At last the bolts grated back, there was a pause, and then the door opened a little way, and Otto thought that he could see someone peeping in from without. By and by the door opened further, there was another pause, and then a slender, elfish-looking little girl, with straight black hair and shining black eyes, crept noiselessly into the room.

She stood close by the door with her finger in her mouth, staring at the boy where he lay upon his couch, and Otto upon his part lay, full of wonder, gazing back upon the little elfin creature.

She, seeing that he made no sign or motion, stepped a little nearer, and then, after a moment's pause, a little nearer still, until, at last, she stood within a few feet of where he lay.

"Art thou the Baron Otto?" said she.

"Yes," answered Otto.

"Prut!" said she, "and is that so! Why, I thought that thou wert a great tall fellow at least, and here thou art a little boy no older than Carl Max, the gooseherd." Then, after a little pause - "My name is Pauline, and my father is the Baron. I heard him tell my mother all about thee, and so I wanted to come here and see thee myself: Art thou sick?"

"Yes," said Otto, "I am sick."

"And did my father hurt thee?"

"Aye," said Otto, and his eyes filled with tears, until one sparkling drop trickled slowly down his white face.

Little Pauline stood looking seriously at him for a while. "I am sorry for thee, Otto," said she, at last. And then, at her childish pity, he began crying in earnest.

This was only the first visit of many from the little maid, for after that she often came to Otto's prison, who began to look for her coming from day to day as the one bright spot in the darkness and the gloom.

Sitting upon the edge of his bed and gazing into his face with wide open eyes, she would listen to him by the hour, as he told her of his life in that far away monastery home; of poor, simple brother John's wonderful visions, of the good Abbot's books with their beautiful pictures, and of all the monkish tales and stories of knights and dragons and heroes and emperors of ancient Rome, which brother Emmanuel had taught him to read in the crabbed monkish Latin in which they were written.

One day the little maid sat for a long while silent after he had ended speaking. At last she drew a deep breath. "And are all these things that thou tellest me about the priests in their castle really true? " said she.

"Yes," said Otto, "all are true."

"And do they never go out to fight other priests?"

"No," said Otto, "they know nothing of fighting."

"So!" said she. And then fell silent in the thought of the wonder of it all, and that there should be men in the world that knew nothing of violence and bloodshed; for in all the eight years of her life she had scarcely been outside of the walls of Castle Trutz-Drachen

At another time it was of Otto's mother that they were speaking.

"And didst thou never see her, Otto?" said the little girl.

"Aye," said Otto, "I see her sometimes in my dreams, and her face always shines so bright that I know she is an angel; for brother John has often seen the dear angels, and he tells me that their faces always shine in that way. I saw her the night thy father hurt me so, for I could not sleep and my head felt as though it would break asunder. Then she came and leaned over me and kissed my forehead, and after that I fell asleep."

"But where did she come from, Otto?" said the little girl.

"From paradise, I think," said Otto, with that patient seriousness that he had caught from the monks, and that sat so quaintly upon him.

"So!" said little Pauline; and then, after a pause, "That is why thy mother kissed thee when thy head ached - because she is an angel. When I was sick my mother bade Gretchen carry me to a far part of the house, because I cried and so troubled her. Did thy mother ever strike thee, Otto?"

"Nay," said Otto.

"Mine hath often struck me," said Pauline.

One day little Pauline came bustling into Otto's cell, her head full of the news which she carried. "My father says that thy father is out in the woods somewhere yonder, back of the castle, for Fritz, the swineherd, told my father that last night he had seen a fire in the woods, and that he had crept up to it without anyone knowing. There he had seen the Baron Conrad and six of his men, and that they were eating one of the swine that they had killed and roasted. "Maybe," said she, seating herself upon the edge of Otto's couch; "maybe my father will kill thy father, and they will bring him here and let him lie upon a black bed with bright candles burning around him, as they did my uncle Frederick when he was killed."

"God forbid!" said Otto, and then lay for a while with his hands clasped. "Dost thou love me, Pauline?" said he, after a while.

"Yes," said Pauline, "for thou art a good child, though my father says that thy wits are cracked."

"Mayhap they are," said Otto, simply, "for I have often been told so before. But thou wouldst not see me die, Pauline; wouldst thou?"

"Nay," said Pauline, "I would not see thee die, for then thou couldst tell me no more stories; for they told me that uncle Frederick could not speak because he was dead."

"Then listen, Pauline," said Otto; "if I go not away from here I shall surely die. Every day I grow more sick and the leech cannot cure me." Here he broke down and, turning his face upon the couch, began crying, while little Pauline sat looking seriously at him.

"Why dost thou cry, Otto?" said she, after a while.

"Because," said he, "I am so sick, and I want my father to come and take me away from here."

"But why dost thou want to go away?" said Pauline. "If thy father takes thee away, thou canst not tell me any more stories."

"Yes, I can," said Otto, "for when I grow to be a man I will come again and marry thee, and when thou art my wife I can tell thee all the stories that I know. Dear Pauline, canst thou not tell my father where I am, that he may come here and take me away before I die?"

"Mayhap I could do so," said Pauline, after a little while, "for sometimes I go with Casper Max to see his mother, who nursed me when I was a baby. She is the wife of Fritz, the swineherd, and she will make him tell thy father; for she will do whatever I ask of her, and Fritz will do whatever she bids him do."

"And for my sake, wilt thou tell him, Pauline?" said Otto.

"But see, Otto," said the little girl, "if I tell him, wilt thou promise to come indeed and marry me when thou art grown a man?"

Yes," said Otto, very seriously, " I will promise."

"Then I will tell thy father where thou art," said she.

"But thou wilt do it without the Baron Henry knowing, wilt thou not, Pauline?"

"Yes," said she, "for if my father and my mother knew that I did such a thing, they would strike me, mayhap send me to my bed alone in the dark."

Chapter - IX

How One-eyed Hans came to Trutz-Drachen

Fritz, the swineherd, sat eating his late supper of porridge out of a great, coarse, wooden bowl; wife Katherine sat at the other end of the table, and the half-naked little children played upon the earthen floor. A shaggy dog lay curled up in front of the fire, and a grunting pig scratched against a leg of the rude table close beside where the woman sat.

"Yes, yes," said Katherine, speaking of the matter of which they had already been talking. "It is all very true that the Drachenhausens are a bad lot, and I for one am of no mind to say no to that; all the same it is a sad thing that a simple-witted little child like the young Baron should be so treated as the boy has been; and now that our Lord Baron has served him so that he, at least, will never be able to do us 'harm, I for one say that he should not be left there to die alone in that black cell."

Fritz, the swineherd, gave a grunt at this without raising his eyes from the bowl.

"Yes, good," said Katherine, "I know what thou meanest, Fritz, and that it is none of my business to be thrusting my finger into the Baron's dish. But to hear the way that dear little child spoke when she was here this morn - it would have moved a heart of stone to hear her tell of all his pretty talk. Thou wilt try to let the red-beard know that that poor boy, his son, is sick to death in the black cell; wilt thou not, Fritz?"

The swineherd dropped his wooden spoon into the bowl with a clatter. "Potstausand!" he cried; "art thou gone out of thy head to let thy wits run upon such things as this of which thou talkest to me? If it should come to our

FRITZ, THE SWINEHERD, SAT EATING HIS LATE SUPPER OF PORRIDGE.

Lord Baron's ears he would cut the tongue from out thy head and my head from off my shoulders for it. Dost thou think I am going to meddle in such a matter as this ? Listen! these proud Baron folk, with their masterful ways, drive our sort hither and thither; they beat us, they drive us, they kill us as they choose. Our lives are not as much to them as one of my black swine. Why should I trouble my head if they choose to lop and trim one another?

The fewer there are of them the better for us, say I. We poor folk have a hard enough life of it without thrusting our heads into the noose to help them out of their troubles. What thinkest thou would happen to us if Baron Henry should hear of our betraying his affairs to the Red-beard?"

"Nay," said Katherine, "thou hast naught to do in the matter but to tell the Red-beard in what part of the castle the little Baron lies."

"And what good would that do?" said Fritz, the swineherd.

"I know not," said Katherine, "but I have promised the little one that thou wouldst find the Baron Conrad and tell him that much."

"Thou hast promised a mare's egg," said her husband, angrily. "How shall I find the Baron Conrad to bear a message to him, when our Baron has been looking for him in vain for two days past?"

"Thou has found him once and thou mayst find him again," said Katherine, "for it is not likely that he will keep far away from here whilst his boy is in such sore need of help."

"I will have nothing to do with it!" said Fritz, and he got up from the wooden block whereon he was sitting and stumped out of the house. But, then, Katherine had heard him talk in that way before, and knew, in spite of his saying "no," that, sooner or later, he would do as she wished.

Two days later a very stout little one-eyed man, clad in a leathern jerkin and wearing a round leathern cap upon his head, came toiling up the path to the postern door of Trutz-Drachen, his back bowed under the burthen of a great peddler's pack. It was our old friend the one-eyed Hans, though even his brother would hardly have known him in his present guise, for, besides having turned peddler, he had grown of a sudden surprisingly fat.

Rap-tap-tap! He knocked at the door with a knotted end of the crooked thorned staff upon which he leaned. He waited for a while and then knocked again - rap-tap-tap!

Presently, with a click, a little square wicket that pierced the door was opened, and a woman's face peered out through the iron bars.

The one-eyed Hans whipped off his leathern cap.

"Good day, pretty one," said he, "and hast thou any need of glass beads, ribbons, combs, or trinkets? Here I am come all the way from Gruenstadt, with a pack full of such gay things as thou never laid eyes on before. Here be rings and bracelets and necklaces that might be of pure silver and set with diamonds and rubies, for anything that thy dear one could tell if he saw thee decked in them. And all are so cheap that thou hast only to say, 'I want them,' and they are thine."

The frightened face at the window looked from right to left and from left to right. "Hush," said the girl, and laid her finger upon her lips. "There! thou hadst best get away from here, poor soul, as fast as thy legs can carry thee, for if the Lord Baron should find thee here talking secretly at the postern door, he would loose the wolf-hounds upon thee."

"Prut," said one-eyed Hans, with a grin, "the Baron is too big a fly to see such a little gnat as I; but wolf-hounds or no wolf- hounds, I can never go hence without showing thee the pretty things that I have brought from the town, even though my stay be at the danger of my own hide."

HANS HELD UP A NECKLACE OF BLUE AND WHITE BEADS.

He flung the pack from off his shoulders as he spoke and fell to unstrapping it, while the round face of the lass (her eyes big with curiosity) peered down at him through the grated iron bars.

Hans held up a necklace of blue and white beads that glistened like jewels in the sun, and from them hung a gorgeous filigree cross. "Didst thou ever see a sweeter thing than this?" said he; "and look, here is a comb that even the silversmith would swear was pure silver all the way through." Then, in a soft, wheedling voice, "Canst thou not let me in, my little bird? Sure there are other lasses besides thyself who would like to trade with a poor peddler who has travelled all the way from Gruenstadt just to please the pretty ones of Trutz-Drachen."

"Nay," said the lass, in a frightened voice, " I cannot let thee in; I know not what the Baron would do to me, even now, if he knew that I was here talking to a stranger at the postern;" and she made as if she would clap to the little window in his face; but the one-eyed Hans thrust his staff betwixt the bars and so kept the shutter open.

"Nay, nay," said he, eagerly, "do not go away from me too soon. Look, dear one; seest thou this necklace?"

"Aye," said she, looking hungrily at it.

"Then listen; if thou wilt but let me into the castle, so that I may strike a trade, I will give it to thee for thine own without thy paying a barley corn for it."

The girl looked and hesitated, and then looked again; the temptation was too great. There was a noise of softly drawn bolts and bars, the door was hesitatingly opened a little way, and, in a twinkling, the one-eyed Hans had slipped inside the castle, pack and all.

"The necklace," said the girl, in a frightened whisper.

Hans thrust it into her hand. "It's thine," said he, "and now wilt thou not help me to a trade?"

"I will tell my sister that thou art here," said she, and away she ran from the little stone hallway, carefully bolting and locking the further door behind her.

The door that the girl had locked was the only one that connected the postern hail with the castle.

The one-eyed Hans stood looking after her. "Thou fool!" he muttered to himself, "to lock the door behind thee. What shall I do next, I should like to know? Here am I just as badly off as I was when I stood outside the walls. Thou hussy! If thou hadst but let me into the castle for only two little minutes, I would have found somewhere to have hidden myself while thy back was turned. But what shall I do now?" He rested his pack upon the floor and stood looking about him.

Built in the stone wall opposite to him, was a high, narrow fireplace without carving of any sort. As Hans' one eye wandered around the bare stone space, his glance fell at last upon it, and there it rested. For a while he stood looking intently at it, presently he began rubbing his hand over his bristling chin in a thoughtful, meditative manner. Finally he drew a deep breath, and giving himself a shake as though to arouse himself from his thoughts, and after listening a moment or two to make sure that no one was nigh, he walked softly to the fireplace, and stooping, peered up the chimney. Above him yawned a black cavernous depth, inky with the soot of years. Hans straightened himself, and tilting his leathern cap to one side, began scratching his bullet-head; at last he drew a long breath. "Yes, good," he muttered to himself; "he who jumps into the river must e'en swim the best he can. It is a vile, dirty place to thrust one's self; but I am in for it now, and must make the best of a lame horse."

He settled the cap more firmly upon his head, spat upon his hands, and once more stooping in the fireplace, gave a leap, and up the chimney he went with a rattle of loose mortar and a black trickle of soot.

By and by footsteps sounded outside the door. There was a pause; a hurried whispering of women's voices; the twitter of a nervous laugh, and then the door was pushed softly opens and the girl to whom the one-eyed Hans had given the necklace of blue and white beads with the filigree cross hanging from it, peeped uncertainly into the room. Behind her broad, heavy face were three others, equally homely and stolid; for a while all four stood there, looking blankly into the room and around it. Nothing was there but the peddler's knapsack lying in the middle of the floor-the man was gone. The light of expectancy slowly faded Out of the girl's face, and in its place succeeded first bewilderment and then dull alarm. "But, dear heaven," she said, "where then has the peddler man gone?"

A moment or two of silence followed her speech. "Perhaps," said one of the others, in a voice hushed with awe, "perhaps it was the evil one himself to whom thou didst open the door."

Again there was a hushed and breathless pause; it was the lass who had let Hans in at the postern, who next spoke.

"Yes," said she, in a voice trembling with fright at what she had done, "yes, it must have been the evil one, for now I remember he had but one eye." The four girls crossed themselves, and their eyes grew big and round with the fright.

Suddenly a shower of mortar came rattling down the chimney. "Ach!" cried the four, as with one voice. Bang! the door was clapped to and away they scurried like a flock of frightened rabbits.

When Jacob, the watchman, came that way an hour later, upon his evening round of the castle, he found a peddler's knapsack lying in the middle of the floor. He turned it over with his pike-staff and saw that it was full of beads and trinkets and ribbons.

"How came this here?" said he. And then, without waiting for the answer which he did not expect, he flung it over his shoulder and marched away with it

Chapter - X

How Hans Brought Terror to the Kitchen

Hans found himself in a pretty pickle in the chimney, for the soot got into his one eye and set it to watering, and into his nose and set him to sneezing, and into his mouth and his ears and his hair. But still he struggled on, up and up; "for every chimney has a top," said Hans to himself "and I am sure to climb out somewhere or other." Suddenly he came to a place where another chimney joined the one he was climbing, and here he stopped to consider the matter at his leisure. "See now," he muttered, "if I still go upward I may come out at the top of some tall chimney-stack with no way of getting down outside. Now, below here there must be a fire-place somewhere, for a chimney does not start from nothing at all; yes, good! we will go down a while and see what we make of that."

It was a crooked, zigzag road that he had to travel, and rough and hard into the bargain. His one eye tingled and smarted, and his knees and elbows were rubbed to the quick; nevertheless One- eyed Hans had been in worse trouble than this in his life.

Down he went and down he went, further than he had climbed upward before. "Sure, I must be near some place or other," he thought.

As though in instant answer to his thoughts, he heard the sudden sound of a voice so close beneath him that he stopped short in his downward climbing and stood as still as a mouse, with his heart in his mouth. A few inches more and he would have been discovered; - what would have happened then would have been no hard matter to foretell.

Hans braced his back against one side of the chimney, his feet against the other and then, leaning forward, looked down between his knees. The gray light of the coming evening glimmered in a wide stone fireplace just below him. Within the fireplace two people were moving about upon the broad hearth, a great, fat woman and a shock-headed boy. The woman held a spit with two newly trussed fowls upon it, so that One-eyed Hans knew that she must be the cook.

"THOU UGLY TOAD," SAID THE WOMAN.

"Thou ugly toad," said the woman to the boy, "did I not bid thee make a fire an hour ago? and now, here there is not so much as a spark to roast the fowls withall, and they to be basted for the lord Baron's supper. Where hast thou been for all this time?"

No matter," said the boy, sullenly, as he laid the fagots ready for the lighting; "no matter, I was not running after Long Jacob, the bowman, to try to catch him for a sweetheart, as thou hast been doing."

The reply was instant and ready. The cook raised her hand; "smack!" she struck and a roar from the scullion followed.

"Yes, good," thought Hans, as he looked down upon them; "I am glad that the boy's ear was not on my head."

"Now give me no more of thy talk," said the woman, "but do the work that thou hast been bidden." Then - "How came all this black soot here, I should like to know?"

"How should I know?" snuffled the scullion, "mayhap thou wouldst blame that on me also?"

"That is my doing," whispered Hans to himself; "but if they light the fire, what then becomes of me?"

"See now," said the cook; "I go to make the cakes ready; if I come back and find that thou hast not built the fire, I will warm thy other ear for thee."

"So," thought Hans; "then will be my time to come down the chimney, for there will be but one of them."

The next moment he heard the door close and knew that the cook had gone to make the cakes ready as she said. And as he looked down he saw that the boy was bending over the bundle of fagots, blowing the spark that he had brought in upon the punk into a flame. The dry fagots began to crackle and blaze. "Now is my time," said Hans to himself. Bracing his elbows against each side of the chimney, he straightened his legs so that he might fall clear His motions loosened little shower of soot that fell rattling upon the fagots that were now beginning to blaze brightly, whereupon the boy raised his face and looked up. Hans loosened his hold upon the chimney; crash! he fell, lighting upon his feet in the midst of the burning fagots. The scullion boy tumbled backward upon the floor, where he lay upon the broad of his back with a face as white as dough and eyes and mouth agape, staring speechlessly at the frightful inky-black figure standing in the midst of the flames and smoke. Then his scattered wits came back to him. "It is the evil one," he roared. And thereupon, turning upon his side, he half rolled, half scrambled to the door. Then out he leaped and, banging it to behind him, flew down the passageway, yelling with fright and never daring once to look behind him.

All the time One-eyed Hans was brushing away the sparks that clung to his clothes. He was as black as ink from head to foot with the soot from the chimney.

"So far all is good," he muttered to himself, "but if I go wandering about in my sooty shoes I will leave black tracks to follow me, so there is nothing to do but e'en to go barefoot. He stooped and drawing the pointed soft leather shoes from his feet, he threw them upon the now blazing fagots, where they writhed and twisted and wrinkled, and at last burst into a flame. Meanwhile Hans lost no time; he must find a hiding-place, and quickly, if he would yet hope to escape. A great bread trough stood in the corner of the kitchen - a hopper-shaped chest with a flat lid. It was the best hiding place that the room afforded. Without further thought Hans ran to it, snatching up from the table as he passed a loaf of black bread and a bottle half full of stale wine, for he had had nothing to eat since that morning. Into the great bread trough he climbed, and drawing the lid down upon him, curled himself up as snugly as a mouse in its nest.

For a while the kitchen lay in silence, but at last the sound of voices was heard at the door, whispering together in low tones. Suddenly the door was flung open and a tall, lean, lantern-jawed fellow, clad in rough frieze, strode into the room and stood there glaring with half frightened boldness around about him; three or four women and the trembling scullion crowded together in a frightened group behind him.

The man was Long Jacob, the bowman; but, after all, his boldness was all wasted, for not a thread or a hair was to be seen, but only the crackling fire throwing its cheerful ruddy glow upon the wall of the room, now rapidly darkening in the falling gray of the twilight without.

The fat cook's fright began rapidly to turn into anger.

"Thou imp," she cried, "it is one of thy tricks," and she made a dive for the scullion, who ducked around the skirts of one of the other women and so escaped for the time; but Long Jacob wrinkled up his nose and sniffed. "Nay," said he, "me thinks that there lieth some truth in the tale that the boy hath told, for here is a vile smell of burned horn that the black one hath left behind him."

It was the smell from the soft leather shoes that Hans had burned.

The silence of night had fallen over the Castle of Trutz- Drachen; not a sound was heard but the squeaking of mice scurring behind the wainscoting, the dull dripping of moisture from the eaves, or the sighing of the night wind around the gables and through the naked windows of the castle.

The lid of the great dough trough was softly raised, and a face, black with soot, peeped cautiously out from under it. Then little by little arose a figure as black as the face; and One- eyed Hans stepped out upon the floor, stretching and rubbing himself.

"Methinks I must have slept," he muttered. " Hui, I am as stiff as a new leather doublet, and now, what next is to become of me? I hope my luck may yet stick to me, in spite of this foul black soot!"

Along the middle of the front of the great hall of the castle, ran a long stone gallery, opening at one end upon the court-yard by a high flight of stone steps. A man-at-arms in breast-plate and steel cap, and bearing a long pike, paced up and down the length of this gallery, now and then stopping, leaning over the edge, and gazing up into the starry sky above; then, with a long drawn yawn, lazily turning back to the monotonous watch again.

THE MAN WAS LONG JACOB, THB BOWMAN.

A dark figure crept out from an arched doorway at the lower part of the long straight building, and some little distance below the end gallery, but the sentry saw nothing of it, for his back was turned. As silently and as stealthily as a cat the figure crawled along by the dark shadowy wall, now and then stopping, and then again creeping slowly forward toward the gallery where the man-at-arms moved monotonously up and down. It was One-eyed Hans in his bare feet.

Inch by inch, foot by foot - the black figure crawled along in the angle of the wall; inch by inch and foot by foot, but ever nearer and nearer to the long straight row of stone steps that led to the covered gallery. At last it crouched at the lowest step of the flight. Just then the sentinel upon watch came to the very end of the gallery and stood there leaning upon his spear. Had he looked down below he could not have failed to have seen One-eyed Hans lying there motionlessly; but he was gazing far away over the steep black roofs beyond, and never saw the unsuspected presence. Minute after minute passed, and the one stood there looking out into the night and the other lay crouching by the wall; then with a weary sigh the sentry turned and began slowly pacing back again toward the farther end of the gallery.

Instantly the motionless figure below arose and glided noiselessly and swiftly up the flight of steps.

Two rude stone pillars flanked either side of the end of the gallery. Like a shadow the black figure slipped behind one of these, flattening itself up against the wall, where it stood straight and motionless as the shadows around it.

Down the long gallery came the watchman, his sword clinking loudly in the silence as he walked, tramp, tramp, tramp! clink, clank, jingle.

Within three feet of the motionless figure behind the pillar he turned, and began retracing his monotonous steps. Instantly the other left the shadow of the post and crept rapidly and stealthily after him. One step, two steps the sentinel took; for a moment the black figure behind him seemed to crouch and draw together, then like a flash it leaped forward upon its victim.

A shadowy cloth fell upon the man's face, and in an instant he was flung back and down with a muffled crash upon the stones. Then followed a fierce and silent struggle in the darkness, but strong and sturdy as the man was, he was no match for the almost superhuman strength of One-eyed Hans. The cloth which he had flung over his head was tied tightly and securely. Then the man was forced upon his face and, in spite of his fierce struggles, his arms were bound around and around with strong fine cord; next his feet were bound in the same way, and the task was done. Then Hans stood upon his feet, and wiped the sweat from his swarthy forehead. "Listen, brother," he whispered, and as he spoke he stooped and pressed something cold and hard against the neck of the other. "Dost thou know the feel of this? It is a broad dagger, and if

IN AN INSTANT HE WAS FLUNG BACK AND DOWN.

thou dost contrive to loose that gag from thy mouth and makest any outcry, it shall be sheathed in thy weasand."

So saying, he thrust the knife back again into its sheath, then stooping and picking up the other, he flung him across his shoulder like a sack, and running down the steps as lightly as though his load was nothing at all, he carried his burden to the arched doorway whence he had come a little while before. There, having first stripped his prisoner of all his weapons, Hans sat the man up in the angle of the wall. "So, brother;" said he, "now we can talk with more ease than we could up yonder. I will tell thee frankly why I am here; it is to find where the young Baron Otto of Drachenhausen is kept. If thou canst tell me, well and good; if not, I must e'en cut thy weasand and find me one who knoweth more. Now, canst thou tell me what I would learn, brother?"

The other nodded dimly in the darkness.

"That is good," said Hans, "then I will loose thy gag until thou hast told me; only bear in mind what I said concerning my dagger."

Thereupon, he unbound his prisoner, and the fellow slowly rose to his feet. He shook himself and looked all about him in a heavy, bewildered fashion, as though he had just awakened from a dream.

His right hand slid furtively down to his side, but the dagger- sheath was empty.

"Come, brother!" said Hans, impatiently, "time is passing, and once lost can never be found again. Show me the way to the young Baron Otto or -." And he whetted the shining blade of his dagger on his horny palm.

The fellow needed no further bidding; turning, he led the way, and together they were swallowed up in the yawning shadows, and again the hush of night-time lay upon the Castle of Trutz- Drachen.

Chapter - XI

How Otto was Saved

Little Otto was lying upon the hard couch in his cell, tossing in restless and feverish sleep; suddenly a heavy hand was laid upon him and a voice whispered in his ear, "Baron, Baron Otto, waken, rouse yourself; I am come to help you. I am One-eyed Hans."

Otto was awake in an instant and raised himself upon his elbow in the darkness. "One-eyed Hans," he breathed, "One-eyed Hans; who is One-eyed Hans?"

"True," said the other, "thou dost not know me. I am thy father's trusted servant, and am the only one excepting his own blood and kin who has clung to him in this hour of trouble. Yes, all are gone but me alone, and so I have come to help thee away from this vile place."

"Oh, dear, good Hans! if only thou canst!" cried Otto; "if only thou canst take me away from this wicked place. Alas, dear Hans! I am weary and sick to death." And poor little Otto began to weep silently in the darkness.

"Aye, aye," said Hans, gruffly, "it is no place for a little child to be. Canst thou climb, my little master? canst thou climb a knotted rope?"

"Nay," said Otto, "I can never climb again! See, Hans;" and he flung back the covers from off him.

"I cannot see," said Hans, "it is too dark."

"Then feel, dear Hans," said Otto.

Hans bent over the poor little white figure glimmering palely in the darkness. Suddenly he drew back with a snarl like an angry wolf. "Oh! the black, bloody wretches!" he cried, hoarsely; "and have they done that to thee, a little child?"

"Yes," said Otto, "the Baron Henry did it." And then again he began to cry.

"There, there," said Hans, roughly, "weep no more. Thou shalt get away from here even if thou canst not climb; I myself will help thee. Thy father is already waiting below the window here, and thou shalt soon be with him. There, there, cry no more."

While he was speaking Hans had stripped off his peddler's leathern jacket, and there, around his body, was wrapped coil after coil of stout hempen rope tied in knots at short distances. He began unwinding the rope, and when he had done he was as thin as ever he had been before. Next he drew from the pouch that hung at his side a ball of fine cord and a leaden weight pierced by a hole, both of which he had brought with him for the use to which he now put them. He tied the lead to the end of the cord, then whirling the weight above his head, he flung it up toward the window high above. Twice the piece of lead fell back again into the room; the third time it flew out between the iron bars carrying the cord with it. Hans held the ball in his hand and paid out the string as the weight carried it downward toward the ground beneath. Suddenly the cord stopped running. Hans jerked it and shook it, but it moved no farther. "Pray heaven, little child," said he, "that it hath reached the ground, for if it hath not we are certainly lost."

"I do pray," said Otto, and he bowed his head.

Then, as though in answer to his prayer, there came a twitch upon the cord.

"See," said Hans, "they have heard thee up above in heaven; it was thy father who did that." Quickly and deftly he tied the cord to the end of the knotted rope; then he gave an answering jerk upon the string. The next moment the rope was drawn up to the window and down the outside by those below. Otto lay watching the rope as it crawled up to the window and out into the night like a great snake, while One-eyed Hans held the other end lest it should be drawn too far. At last it stopped. "Good," muttered Hans, as though to himself. "The rope is long enough."

He waited for a few minutes and then, drawing upon the rope and finding that it was held from below, he spat upon his hands and began slowly climbing up to the window above. Winding his arm around the iron bars of the grating that guarded it, he thrust his hand into the pouch that hung by his side, and drawing forth a file, fell to work cutting through all that now lay between Otto and liberty.

It was slow, slow work, and it seemed to Otto as though Hans would never finish his task, as lying upon his hard couch he watched that figure, black against the sky, bending over its work. Now and then the file screeched against the hard iron, and then Hans would cease for a moment, but only to begin again as industriously as ever. Three or four times he tried the effects of his work, but still the iron held. At last he set his shoulder against it, and as

THE NEXT MOMENT THEY WERE HANGING IN MID-AIR.

Otto looked he saw the iron bend. Suddenly there was a sharp crack, and a piece of the grating went flying out into the night.

Hans tied the rope securely about the stump of the stout iron bar that yet remained, and then slid down again into the room below.

"My little lord," said he, "dost thou think that if I carry thee, thou wilt be able and strong enough to cling to my neck?"

"Aye," said Otto, "methinks I will be able to do that."

"Then come," said Hans.

He stooped as he spoke, and gently lifting Otto from his rude and rugged bed he drew his broad leathern belt around them both, buckling it firmly and securely. "It does not hurt thee?" said he.

"Not much," whispered Otto faintly.

Then Hans spat upon his hands, and began slowly climbing the rope.

They reached the edge of the window and there they rested for a moment, and Otto renewed his hold around the neck of the faithful Hans.

"And now art thou ready?" said Hans

"Aye," said Otto.

"Then courage," said Hans, and he turned and swung his leg over the abyss below.

The next moment they were hanging in mid-air.

Otto looked down and gave a gasp. "The mother of heaven bless us," he whispered, and then closed his eyes, faint and dizzy at the sight of that sheer depth beneath. Hans said nothing, but shutting his teeth and wrapping his legs around the rope, he began slowly descending, hand under hand. Down, down, down he went, until to Otto, with his eyes shut and his head leaning upon Hans' shoulder, it seemed as though it could never end. Down, down, down. Suddenly he felt Hans draw a deep breath; there was a slight jar, and Otto opened his eyes; Hans was standing upon the ground.

A figure wrapped in a dark cloak arose from the shadow of the wall, and took Otto in its arms. It was Baron Conrad.

"My son - my little child!" he cried, in a choked, trembling voice, and that was all. And Otto pressed his cheek against his father's and began crying.

Suddenly the Baron gave a sharp, fierce cry. "Dear Heaven!" he cried; "what have they done to thee?" But poor little Otto could not answer.

"Oh!" gasped the Baron, in a strangled voice, "my little child! my little child!" And therewith he broke down, and his whole body shook with fierce, dry sobs; for men in those days did not seek to hide their grief as they do now, but were fierce and strong in the expression of that as of all else.

"Never mind, dear father," whispered Otto; "it did not hurt me so very much," and he pressed his lips against his father's cheek.

Little Otto had but one hand.

Chapter - XII

A Ride For Life

But not yet was Otto safe, and all danger past and gone by. Suddenly, as they stood there, the harsh clangor of a bell broke the silence of the starry night above their heads, and as they raised their faces and looked up, they saw lights flashing from window to window. Presently came the sound of a hoarse voice shouting something that, from the distance, they could not understand.

One-eyed Hans smote his hand upon his thigh. Look said he, "here is what comes of having a soft heart in one's bosom. I overcame and bound a watchman up yonder, and forced him to tell me where our young Baron lay. It was on my mind to run my knife into him after he had told me every thing, but then, bethinking how the young Baron hated the thought of bloodshed, I said to myself, 'No, Hans, I will spare the villain's life.' See now what comes of being merciful; here, by hook or by crook, the fellow has loosed himself from his bonds, and brings the whole castle about our ears like a nest of wasps."

"We must fly," said the Baron; "for nothing else in the world is left me, now that all have deserted me in this black time of trouble, excepting these six faithful ones."

His voice was bitter, bitter, as he spoke; then stooping, he raised Otto in his arms, and bearing him gently, began rapidly descending the rocky slope to the level road that ran along the edge of the hill beneath. Close behind him followed the rest; Hans still grimed with soot and in his bare feet. A little distance from the road and under the shade of the forest trees, seven horses stood waiting. The Baron mounted upon his great black charger, seating little Otto upon the saddle in front of him. "Forward!" he cried, and away they clattered and out upon the road. Then - "To St. Michaelsburg," said Baron Conrad, in his deep voice, and the horses' heads were turned to the westward, and away they galloped through the black shadows of the forest, leaving Trutz-Drachen behind them.

But still the sound of the alarm bell rang through the beating of the horses' hoofs, and as Hans looked over his shoulder, he saw the light of torches flashing hither and thither along the outer walls in front of the great barbican.

In Castle Trutz-Drachen all was confusion and uproar: flashing torches lit up the dull gray walls; horses neighed and stamped, and men shouted and called to one another in the bustle of making ready. Presently Baron Henry came striding along the corridor clad in light armor, which he had hastily donned when roused from his sleep by the news that his prisoner had escaped. Below in the courtyard his horse was standing, and without waiting for assistance, he swung himself into the saddle. Then away they all rode and down the steep path, armor ringing, swords clanking, and iron-shod hoofs striking sparks of fire from the hard stones. At their head rode Baron Henry; his triangular shield hung over his shoulder, and in his hand he bore a long, heavy, steel-pointed lance with a pennant flickering darkly from the end.

At the high-road at the base of the slope they paused, for they were at a loss to know which direction the fugitives had taken; a half a score of the retainers leaped from their horses, and began hurrying about hither and thither, and up and down, like hounds searching for the lost scent, and all the time Baron Henry sat still as a rock in the midst of the confusion.

Suddenly a shout was raised from the forest just beyond the road; they had come upon the place where the horses had been tied. It was an easy matter to trace the way that Baron Conrad and his followers had taken thence back to the high-road, but there again they were at a loss. The road ran straight as an arrow eastward and westward - had the fugitives taken their way to the east or to the west?

Baron Henry called his head-man, Nicholas Stein, to him, and the two spoke together for a while in an undertone. At last the Baron's lieutenant reined his horse back, and choosing first one and then another, divided the company into two parties. The baron placed himself at the head of one band and Nicholas Stein at the head of the other. "Forward!" he cried, and away clattered the two companies of horsemen in opposite directions.

It was toward the westward that Baron Henry of Trutz-Drachen rode at the head of his men.

The early springtide sun shot its rays of misty, yellow light across the rolling tops of the forest trees where the little birds were singing in the glory of the May morning. But Baron Henry and his followers thought nothing of the beauty of the peaceful day, and heard nothing of the multitudinous sound of the singing birds as, with a confused sound of galloping hoofs, they swept along the highway, leaving behind them a slow- curling, low-trailing cloud of dust.

As the sun rose more full and warm, the misty wreaths began to dissolve, until at last they parted and rolled asunder like a white curtain and there,

HE WAS GAZING STRAIGHT BEFORE HIM WITH A SET AND STONY FACE.

before the pursuing horsemen, lay the crest of the mountain toward which they were riding, and up which the road wound steeply.

"Yonder they are, cried a sudden voice behind Baron Henry of Trutz-Drachen, and at the cry all looked upward.

Far away upon the mountain-side curled a cloud of dust, from the midst of which came the star-like flash of burnished armor gleaming in the sun.

Baron Henry said never a word, but his lips curled in a grim smile.

And as the mist wreaths parted One-eyed Hans looked behind and down into the leafy valley beneath. "Yonder they come," said he. "They have followed sharply to gain so much upon us, even though our horses are wearied with all the travelling we have done hither and yon these five days past. How far is it, Lord Baron, from here to Michaelsburg?"

"About ten leagues," said the Baron, in a gloomy voice.

Hans puckered his mouth as though to whistle, but the Baron saw nothing of it, for he was gazing straight before him with a set and stony face. Those who followed him looked at one another, and the same thought was in the mind of each - how long would it be before those who pursued would close the distance between them?

When that happened it meant death to one and all.

They reached the crest of the hill, and down they dashed upon the other side; for there the road was smooth and level as it sloped away into the valley, but it was in dead silence that they rode. Now and then those who followed the Baron looked back over their shoulders. They had gained a mile upon their pursuers when the helmeted heads rose above the crest of the mountain, but what was the gain of a mile with a smooth road between them, and fresh horses to weary ones?

On they rode and on they rode. The sun rose higher and higher, and hotter and hotter. There was no time to rest and water their panting horses. Only once, when they crossed a shallow stretch of water, the poor animals bent their heads and caught a few gulps from the cool stream, and the One-eyed Hans washed a part of the soot from his hands and face. On and on they rode; never once did the Baron Conrad move his head or alter that steadfast look as, gazing straight before him, he rode steadily forward along the endless stretch of road, with poor little Otto's yellow head and white face resting against his steel-clad shoulder - and St. Michaelsburg still eight leagues away.

A little rise of ground lay before them, and as they climbed it, all, excepting the baron, turned their heads as with one accord and looked behind them. Then more than one heart failed, for through the leaves of the trees below, they caught the glint of armor of those who followed - not more than a mile away. The next moment they swept over the crest, and there, below them, lay the broad shining river, and nearer a tributary stream spanned by a rude, narrow, three-arched, stone bridge where the road crossed the deep, slow-moving water.

Down the slope plodded the weary horses, and so to the bridge- head.

"Halt," cried the baron suddenly, and drew rein.

The others stood bewildered. What did he mean to do? He turned to Hans and his blue eyes shone like steel.

"Hans," said he, in his deep voice, "thou hast served me long and truly; wilt thou for this one last time do my bidding?"

"Aye," said Hans, briefly.

"Swear it," said the Baron.

"I swear it," said Hans, and he drew the sign of the cross upon his heart.

"That is good," said the Baron, grimly. "Then take thou this child, and with the others ride with all the speed that thou canst to St. Michaelsburg. Give the child into the charge of the Abbot Otto. Tell him how that I have sworn fealty to the Emperor, and what I have gained thereby - my castle burnt, my people slain, and this poor, simple child, my only son, mutilated by my enemy.

"And thou, my Lord Baron?" said Hans.

"I will stay here," said the Baron, quietly, "and keep back those who follow as long as God will give me grace so to do."

A murmur of remonstrance rose among the faithful few who were with him, two of whom were near of kin. But Conrad of Drachenhausen turned fiercely upon them. "How now," said he, "have I fallen so low in my troubles that even ye dare to raise your voices against me? By the good Heaven, I will begin my work here by slaying the first man who dares to raise word against my bidding." Then he turned from them. "Here, Hans," said he, "take the boy; and remember, knave, what thou hast sworn."

He pressed Otto close to his breast in one last embrace. "My little child," he murmured, "try not to hate thy father when thou thinkest of him hereafter, even though he be hard and bloody as thou knowest."

But with his suffering and weakness, little Otto knew nothing of what was passing; it was only as in a faint flickering dream that he lived in what was done around him.

"Farewell, Otto," said the Baron, but Otto's lips only moved faintly in answer. His father kissed him upon either cheek. "Come, Hans," said he, hastily, "take him hence;" and he loosed Otto's arms from about his neck.

Hans took Otto upon the saddle in front of him.

"Oh! my dear Lord Baron," said he, and then stopped with a gulp, and turned his grotesquely twitching face aside.

"Go," said the Baron, harshly, "there is no time to lose in woman's tears."

"Farewell, Conrad! farewell, Conrad!" said his two kinsmen, and coming forward they kissed him upon the cheek then they turned and rode away after Hans, and Baron Conrad was left alone to face his mortal foe.

Chapter - XIII

How Baron Conrad Held the Bridge

As the last of his followers swept around the curving road and was lost to sight, Baron Conrad gave himself a shake, as though to drive away the thoughts that lay upon him. Then he rode slowly forward to the middle of the bridge, where he wheeled his horse so as to face his coming enemies. He lowered the vizor of his helmet and bolted it to its place, and then saw that sword and dagger were loose in the scabbard and easy to draw when the need for drawing should arise.

Down the steep path from the hill above swept the pursuing horsemen. Down the steep path to the bridge-head and there drew rein; for in the middle of the narrow way sat the motionless, steel-clad figure upon the great war-horse, with wide, red, panting nostrils, and body streaked with sweat and flecked with patches of foam.

One side of the roadway of the bridge was guarded by a low stone wall; the other side was naked and open and bare to the deep, slow-moving water beneath. It was a dangerous place to attack a desperate man clad in armor of proof.

"Forward!" cried Baron Henry, but not a soul stirred in answer, and still the iron-clad figure sat motionless and erect upon the panting horse.

"How," cried the Baron Henry, "are ye afraid of one man? Then follow me!" and he spurred forward to the bridge-head. But still no one moved in answer, and the Lord of Trutz-Drachen reined back his horse again. He wheeled his horse and glared round upon the stolid faces of his followers, until his eyes seemed fairly to blaze with passion beneath the bars of his vizor.

Baron Conrad gave a roar of laughter. "How now," he cried; "are ye all afraid of one man? Is there none among ye that dares come forward and meet me? I know thee, Baron Henry thou art not afraid to cut off the hand of a little child. Hast thou not now the courage to face the father?"

IN THE MIDDLE OF THE NARROW WAY STOOD
THE MOTIONLESS, STEEL-CLAD FIGURE.

Baron Henry gnashed his teeth with rage as he glared around upon the faces of his men-at-arms. Suddenly his eye lit upon one of them. "Ha ! Carl Spigler," he cried, "thou hast thy cross-bow with thee; - shoot me down yonder dog! Nay," he said, "thou canst do him no harm under his armor; shoot the horse upon which he sits."

Baron Conrad heard the speech. "Oh! thou coward villain !" he cried, "stay; do not shoot the good horse. I will dismount and fight ye upon foot." Thereupon, armed as he was, he leaped clashing from his horse and turning the animal's head, gave it a slap upon the flank. The good horse first trotted and then walked to the further end of the bridge, where it stopped and began cropping at the grass that grew beside the road.

"Now then !" cried Baron Henry, fiercely, "now then, ye cannot fear him, villains! Down with him! forward!"

Slowly the troopers spurred their horses forward upon the bridge and toward that one figure that, grasping tightly the great two- handed sword, stood there alone guarding the passage.

Then Baron Conrad whirled the great blade above his head, until it caught the sunlight and flashed again. He did not wait for the attack, but when the first of the advancing horsemen had come within a few feet of him, he leaped with a shout upon them. The fellow thrust at him with his lance, and the Baron went staggering a few feet back, but instantly he recovered himself and again leaped forward. The great sword flashed in the air, whistling; it fell, and the nearest man dropped his lance, clattering, and with a loud, inarticulate cry, grasped the mane of his horse with both hands. Again the blade whistled in the air, and this time it was stained with red. Again it fell, and with another shrill cry the man toppled headlong beneath the horse's feet. The next instant they were upon him, each striving to strike at the one figure, to ride him down, or to thrust him down with their lances. There was no room now to swing the long blade, but holding the hilt in both hands, Baron Conrad thrust with it as though it were a lance, stabbing at horse or man, it mattered not. Crowded upon the narrow roadway of the bridge, those who attacked had not only to guard themselves against the dreadful strokes of that terrible sword, but to keep their wounded horses (rearing and mad with fright) from toppling bodily over with them into the water beneath.

Presently the cry was raised, "Back! back!" And those nearest the Baron began reining in their horses. "Forward!" roared Baron Henry, from the midst of the crowd; but in spite of his command, and even the blows that he gave, those behind were borne back by those in front, struggling and shouting, and the bridge was cleared again excepting for three figures that lay motionless upon the roadway, and that one who, with the brightness of his armor dimmed and stained, leaned panting against the wall of the bridge.

The Baron Henry raged like a madman. Gnashing his teeth together, he rode back a little way; then turning and couching his lance, he suddenly clapped spurs to his horse, and the next instant came thundering down upon his solitary enemy.

Baron Conrad whirled his sword in the air, as he saw the other coming like a thunderbolt upon him; he leaped aside, and the lance passed close to him. As it passed he struck, and the iron point flew from the shaft of the spear at the blow, and fell clattering upon the stone roadway of the bridge.

Baron Henry drew in his horse until it rested upon its haunches, then slowly reined it backward down the bridge, still facing his foe, and still holding the wooden stump of the lance in his hand. At the bridge-head he flung it from him.

"Another lance!" he cried, hoarsely. One was silently reached to him and he took it, his hand trembling with rage. Again he rode to a little distance and wheeled his horse; then, driving his steel spurs into its quivering side, he came again thundering down upon the other. Once more the terrible sword whirled in the air and fell, but this time the lance was snatched to one side and the blow fell harmlessly. The next instant, and with a twitch of the bridle-rein, the horse struck full and fair against the man. Conrad of Drachenhausen was whirled backward and downward, and the cruel iron hoofs crashed over his prostrate body, as horse and man passed with a rush beyond him and to the bridge-head beyond. A shout went up from those who stood watching. The next moment the prostrate figure rose and staggered blindly to the side of the bridge, and stood leaning against the stone wall.

At the further end of the bridge Baron Henry had wheeled his horse. Once again he couched lance, and again he drove down upon his bruised and wounded enemy. This time the lance struck full and fair, and those who watched saw the steel point pierce the iron breast-plate and then snap short, leaving the barbed point within the wound.

Baron Conrad sunk to his knees and the Roderburg, looming upon his horse above him, unsheathed his sword to finish the work he had begun.

Then those who stood looking on saw a wondrous thing happen: the wounded man rose suddenly to his feet, and before his enemy could strike he leaped, with a great and bitter cry of agony and despair, upon him as he sat in the saddle above.

Henry of Trutz-Drachen grasped at his horse's mane, but the attack was so fierce, so sudden, and so unexpected that before he could save himself he was dragged to one side and fell crashing in his armor upon the stone roadway of the bridge.

"The dragon! the dragon!" roared Baron Conrad, in a voice of thunder, and with the energy of despair he dragged his prostrate foe toward the open side of the bridge.

"Forward !" cried the chief of the Trutz-Drachen men, and down they rode upon the struggling knights to the rescue of their master in this new danger. But they were too late.

FOR A MOMENT THEY STOOD SWAYING BACKWARD AND FORWARD.

There was a pause at the edge of the bridge, for Baron Henry had gained his feet and, stunned and bewildered as he was by the suddenness of his fall, he was now struggling fiercely, desperately. For a moment they stood swaying backward and forward, clasped in one another's arms, the blood from the wounded man's breast staining the armor of both. The moment passed and then, with a shower of stones and mortar from beneath their iron-shod heels, they toppled and fell; there was a thunderous splash in the water below, and as the men-at-arms came hurrying up and peered with awe-struck faces over the parapet of the bridge, they saw the whirling eddies sweep down with the current of the stream, a few bubbles rise to the surface of the water, and then - nothing; for the smooth river flowed onward as silently as ever.

Presently a loud voice burst through the awed hush that followed. It came from William of Roderburg, Baron Henry's kinsman. "Forward!" he cried. A murmur of voices from the others was all the answer that he received. "Forward!" cried the young man again, "the boy and those with him are not so far away but that we might yet catch up with them."

Then one of the men spoke up in answer - a man with a seamed, weather-beaten face and crisp grizzled hair. "Nay," said he, "our Lord Baron is gone, and this is no quarrel of ours; here be four of us that are wounded and three I misdoubt that are dead; why should we follow further only to suffer more blows for no gain?" A growl of assent rose from those that stood around, and William of Roderburg saw that nothing more was to be done by the Trutz-Dragons that day.

Chapter - XIV

How Otto Saw the Great Emperor

Through weakness and sickness and faintness, Otto had lain in a half swoon through all that long journey under the hot May sun. It was as in a dreadful nightmare that he had heard on and on and on that monotonous throbbing of galloping hoofs upon the ground; had felt that last kiss that his father had given him upon his cheek. Then the onward ride again, until all faded away into a dull mist and he knew no more. When next he woke it was with the pungent smell of burned vinegar in his nostrils and with the feeling of a cool napkin bathing his brow. He opened his eyes and then closed them again, thinking he must have been in a dream, for he lay in his old room at the peaceful monastery of the White Cross on the hill; the good Father Abbot sat near by, gazing upon his face with the old absent student look, Brother John sat in the deep window seat also gazing at him, and Brother Theodore, the leech of the monastery, sat beside him bathing his head. Beside these old familiar faces were the faces of those who had been with him in that long flight; the One-eyed Hans, old Master Nicholas his kinsman, and the others. So he closed his eyes, thinking that maybe it was all a dream. But the sharp throbbing of the poor stump at his wrist soon taught him that he was still awake.

"Am I then really home in St. Michaelsburg again? he murmured, without unclosing his eyes.

Brother Theodore began snuffling through his nose; there was a pause. "Yes," said the old Abbot at last, and his gentle voice trembled as he spoke; "yes, my dear little child, thou art back again in thine own home; thou hast not been long out in the great world, but truly thou hast had a sharp and bitter trial of it."

"But they will not take me away again, will they?" said Otto quickly, unclosing his blue eyes.

"Nay," said the Abbot, gently; "not until thou art healed in body and art ready and willing to go."

Three months and more had passed, and Otto was well again; and now, escorted by One-eyed Hans and those faithful few who had clung to the Baron Conrad through his last few bitter days, he was riding into the quaint old town of Nurnburg; for the Emperor Rudolph was there at that time, waiting for King Ottocar of Bohemia to come thither and answer the imperial summons before the Council, and Otto was travelling to the court.

As they rode in through the gates of the town, Otto looked up at the high-peaked houses with their overhanging gables, the like of which he had never seen before, and he stared with his round blue eyes at seeing them so crowded together along the length of the street. But most of all he wondered at the number of people that passed hither and thither, jostling each other in their hurry, and at the tradesmen's booths opening upon the street with the wonderful wares hanging within; armor at the smiths, glittering ornaments at the goldsmiths, and rich fabrics of silks and satins at the mercers. He had never seen anything so rich and grand in all of his life, for little Otto had never been in a town before.

"Oh! look," he cried, "at that wonderful lady; see, holy father! sure the Emperor's wife can be no finer than that lady."

The Abbot smiled. "Nay, Otto," said he, "that is but a burgher's wife or daughter; the ladies at the Emperor's court are far grander than such as she."

"So!" said Otto, and then fell silent with wonder.

And now, at last the great moment had come when little Otto with his own eyes was to behold the mighty Emperor who ruled over all the powerful kingdoms of Germany and Austria, and Italy and Bohemia, and other kingdoms and principalities and states. His heart beat so that he could hardly speak as, for a moment, the good Abbot who held him by the hand stopped outside of the arrased doorway to whisper some last instructions into his ear. Then they entered the apartment.

It was a long, stone-paved room. The floor was covered with rich rugs and the walls were hung with woven tapestry wherein were depicted knights and ladies in leafy gardens and kings and warriors at battle. A long row of high glazed windows extended along the length of the apartment, flooding it with the mellow light of the autumn day. At the further end of the room, far away, and standing by a great carved chimney place wherein smouldered the remains of a fire, stood a group of nobles in gorgeous dress of velvet and silks, and with glittering golden chains hung about their necks.

One figure stood alone in front of the great yawning fireplace. His hands were clasped behind him, and his look bent thoughtfully upon the floor. He was dressed only in a simple gray robe without ornament or adornment, a plain leathern belt girded his waist, and from it hung a sword with a bone hilt

IT WAS THE GREAT EMPEROR RUDOLPH.

encased in a brown leathern scabbard. A noble stag-hound lay close behind him, curled up upon the floor, basking in the grateful warmth of the fire.

As the Father Abbot and Otto drew near he raised his head and looked at them. It was a plain, homely face that Otto saw, with a wrinkled forehead and a long mouth drawn down at the corners. It was the face of a good, honest burgher burdened with the cares of a prosperous trade. "Who can he be," thought Otto, "and why does the poor man stand there among all the great nobles?"

But the Abbot walked straight up to him and kneeled upon the floor, and little Otto, full of wonder, did the same. It was the great Emperor Rudolph.

"Who have we here " said the Emperor, and he bent his brow upon the Abbot and the boy.

"Sire," said Abbot Otto, "we have humbly besought you by petition, in the name of your late vassal, Baron Conrad of Vuelph of Drachenhausen, for justice to this his son, the Baron Otto, whom, sire, as you may see, hath been cruelly mutilated at the hands of Baron Henry of Roderburg of Trutz-Drachen. He hath moreover been despoiled of his lands, his castle burnt, and his household made prisoner."

The Emperor frowned until the shaggy eyebrows nearly hid the keen gray twinkle of the eyes beneath. "Yes," said he, "I do remember me of that petition, and have given it consideration both in private and in council." He turned to the group of listening nobles. " Look," said he, "at this little child marred by the inhumanity and the cruelty of those robber villains. By heavens! I will put down their lawless rapine, if I have to give every castle from the north to the south to the flames and to the sword." Then turning to Otto again, "Poor little child," said he, "thy wrongs shall be righted, and so far as they are able, those cruel Roderburgs shall pay thee penny for penny, and grain for grain, for what thou hast lost; and until such indemnity hath been paid the family of the man who wrought this deed shall be held as surety."

Little Otto looked up in the kind, rugged face above him. "Nay, Lord Emperor," said he, in his quaint, quiet way, "there are but two in the family - the mother and the daughter - and I have promised to marry the little girl when she and I are old enough; so, if you please, I would not have harm happen to her."

The Emperor continued to look down at the kneeling boy, and at last he gave a short, dry laugh. "So be it," said he, "thy plan is not without its wisdom. Mayhap it is all for the best that the affair should be ended thus peacefully. The estates of the Roderburgs shall be held in trust for thee until thou art come of age; otherwise it shall be as thou hast proposed, the little maiden shall be taken into ward under our own care. And as to thee - art thou willing that I should take thee under my own charge in the room of thy father, who is dead?"

"Aye," said Otto, simply, "I am willing, for it seems to me that thou art a good man."

The nobles who stood near smiled at the boy's speech. As for the Emperor, he laughed outright. "I give thee thanks, my Lord Baron," said he; "there is no one in all my court who has paid me greater courtesy than that."

So comes the end of our tale.

But perhaps you may like to know what happened afterward, for no one cares to leave the thread of a story without tying a knot in it.

Eight years had passed, and Otto grew up to manhood in the Emperor's court, and was with him through war and peace.

But he himself never drew sword or struck a blow, for the right hand that hung at his side was of pure silver, and the hard, cold fingers never closed. Folks called him "Otto of the Silver Hand," but perhaps there was another reason than that for the name that had been given him, for the pure, simple wisdom that the old monks of the White Cross on the hill had taught him, clung to him through all the honors that the Emperor bestowed upon his favorite, and as he grew older his words were listened to and weighed by those who were high in Council, and even by the Emperor himself.

And now for the end of all.

One day Otto stood uncertainly at the doorway of a room in the imperial castle, hesitating before he entered; and yet there was nothing so very dreadful within, only one poor girl whose heart fluttered more than his. Poor little Pauline, whom he had not seen since that last day in the black cell at Trutz-Drachen.

At last he pushed aside the hangings and entered the room.

She was sitting upon a rude bench beside the window, looking at him out of her great, dark eyes.

He stopped short and stood for a moment confused and silent; for he had no thought in his mind but of the little girl whom he had last seen, and for a moment he stood confused before the fair maiden with her great, beautiful dark eyes.

She on her part beheld a tall, slender youth with curling, golden hair, one hand white and delicate, the other of pure and shining silver.

He came to her and took her hand and set it to his lips, and all that she could do was to gaze with her great, dark eyes upon the hero of whom she had heard so many talk; the favorite of the Emperor; the wise young Otto of the Silver Hand.

HE TOOK HER HAND AND SET IT TO HIS LIPS.

Afterword

The ruins of Drachenhausen were rebuilt, for the walls were as sound as ever, though empty and gaping to the sky; but it was no longer the den of a robber baron for beneath the scutcheon over the great gate was carved a new motto of the Vuelphs; a motto which the Emperor Rudolph himself had given:

"Manus argentea quam manus ferrea melior est"